DIRTY DEBT

LAUREN LANDISH

Edited by
VALORIE CLIFTON
Edited by
STACI E.

LANDISH

DIRTY DEBT

BY LAUREN LANDISH

Sarah Waters was supposed to be a bargaining chip. Nothing more. A pawn for me to use to exact revenge on the man that took everything from me.

But when I look in Sarah's dark mesmerizing eyes, I'm filled with doubt. She has a look of sweet innocence about her that tugs at my hardened heart.

She makes me question if a life of crime is what I want. I'm destined to be the King of the Streets, but I'd give my kingdom away if it meant I could make her mine.

Join my mailing list and receive 2 FREE ebooks!
You'll also be the first to know of new releases, sales,
and giveaways.

CHAPTER 1

RYKER

"He sent word. He's not going to pay. What now?"

I sigh inwardly as I hear my brother, Marcus, over my shoulder. Still, I don't look away from the city skyline. I'm more interested in the streets below than what he just told me. The cars are so small and seemingly so slow beneath me, as if they're merely crawling by in the evening traffic. It's a long way from the streets to up here, but still, I remember those days. I remember the days of scrabbling, of busting my ass and not knowing where the next meal was going to come from.

It gives me an advantage. I'll never forget those days either. I slip my hands into the pockets of my slacks, reminding myself that no matter what else, I won't forget that while the high-up executives of the city might live in penthouses like mine. The heart and

1

blood of this city flows through the asphalt arteries forty-eight floors below me.

"It doesn't matter. I want the most valuable thing he has," I finally answer him. My cold heart barely beats in my chest as I think about the enormity of what I'm asking for. Taking his life is one thing. But men already know that when you don't pay your debt to me, you're dead. Now, it's time to collect on the biggest debt anyone in this city owes me, a debt of blood.

I want to show them all something else, too, something that will truly put fear in their hearts. If my plan is to work, if my dream of vengeance is going to be more than just a short-term coup that ends in disaster, then I need to not only kill Jacob Waters but also strike fear into the heart of every person who stands with him.

Jacob Waters thinks he's untouchable. Or maybe that's what he wants people to assume. He's been in power here in the city for over twenty years. It's hard to think of a time when his name didn't inspire dread in the tight, powerful circles that run this town. I spent most of my childhood knowing and fearing the name of Jacob Waters until that day five years ago when he had our father killed and that fear turned to hate.

Now, it's my turn. I'll kill the bastard, but first, I'm going to destroy him. For twenty years, he's been both the most respected and the most feared man in this state, depending on which side of the law you operate on. No, killing him isn't enough. Before he dies, I'll take everything away from him, piece by piece. I'll make sure everyone he ever relied on turns their back on him as he falls from the highest height that any man in this city can reach. When he's put in the ground, the only attendees are going to be the fucking crows. I want everyone to know the truth.

He's a crime lord. But he's more than that. He's been king of this city for a very long time.

He has the governor, the police commissioner, the judges, and the *fucking law* all in his back pocket. He's made and ended careers, even lives, all with total impunity.

But after two decades, Jacob Waters has gotten arrogant, and he's made a mistake. He might have the judges. He might have the banks. He might have the money and the politicians, and he might even have the corrupt law on his side.

But I have the most important thing on *my* side. I own the streets.

Starting with the tiny little street gang that my father was the shot-caller for. I've grown up in the streets. I ended the turf wars, sometimes through brains and charisma, sometimes with politics, sometimes with muscle, and sometimes with the barrel of a gun. It's taken me five years, but now, I rule the streets.

Better yet, I have leverage on everyone who matters. The cops walk their beats with *my* blessing now. The banks know that their drug money only comes into their accounts because *I* let it. While Jacob's been wining and dining and schmoozing in his mansion up in the Hills, I've been a cancer that eats at him, staying silent until it's time to land the final blow.

I've been waiting for it, biding my time until the time was right. He fucked with the wrong person, and he deserves what's coming to him.

I'm nearly ready for that final blow.

Tonight was the first move in my end game. I had Marcus make a demand for protection money to Salvatore Francisco, one of Jacob's head men. We'll allow him to keep his money laundering racket going on the West Side for a price. Of course, it was rejected, but I already knew that would happen. It was part of my plan. Still, I was worried this morning when I sent Marcus out, knowing that while I've got a strong position, my ass isn't totally covered. And that doesn't make me happy.

"We could take his wife."

My head slowly turns to face Marcus. "What was that, Marcus?"

He shifts from side to side, slightly unsure. I get it. He's not used to being the idea man, even though he's got a good head on his shoulders. But I'm the big brother. I'm the man with the plan, and he's the street lieutenant who gets it done. For him to put forth ideas is unfamiliar territory for him. "I said we could take his wife. You know, that long drink of tall, dark, and sexy that he has on his arm all the time. The ex-actress."

The image of Sarah flashes before my eyes. I can hear her soft laugh, the beautiful cadence of her voice, and the way her hips sway as she moves. It brings back memories of a single day, a perfect moment that still haunts the loneliest of dark nights. For an instant, it makes me pine for her. She's a gorgeous woman and I'm a red-blooded man. But that smile is the same one she makes while she's wrapped in Waters's arms. I clench my jaw and clear my throat, removing the image from my mind.

It's a decent idea, but I need time to think about the consequences. I didn't get to where I am by acting on impulse. "And then what?"

Marcus shrugs. "I dunno, Ryker. I was thinking we could keep her like a human shield. I mean, I know your usual way of doing things—you don't like to get innocents involved—but she's gotta be just as dirty as him. Who the fuck marries a fucker like him unless they're dirty too? She doesn't strike me as being so stupid as to not know. So why not keep her, pretend we're going to rough her up a little, and then let her go?"

It's an inspired idea, honestly. "First his wife, then his business, then his crew, then him? Destroy him bit by bit?"

Marcus nods. "That's what I was thinking. Waters took from us, so we take from him. And you've gotta admit, it's sort of your style."

"My style?" I ask, amused. "And just what is *my* style, Marcus?"

I know he isn't used to so much deep conversation. Most of the time, our conversations are much more direct, lots of yes-or-no type answers. Marcus shifts from side to side again before answering. "It's just . . . you've got flair, man. It's why you do this so much better than me. There's like, a sense of poetry to what you do. And since Waters took Pop from us because of this bitch, maybe it's just sort of fitting that we take from him. Starting with her."

I think about it, and I must admit I'm a little unsure. I have a soft spot for women, but I'm making an example of this fuck-face. I don't care how much power anyone has. No one's going to get away with stealing from me. And Waters stole something more important than money from me. He stole my flesh and blood. He took Pop from us, and he didn't even care. All he cared about was making sure he looked like a tough son of a bitch for someone supposedly flirting with his wife. I even know why Pop maybe, *maybe* could have looked at the woman. She does look a lot like Pop's sister, the aunt who died before I was born. He was probably just taken by how much she looked like her.

It doesn't matter, though. Waters thought that Pop was giving his new bride the horny eye, so he pulled out his gun and POW! I'm twenty-four, parentless since Mom took off when I was a teenager, with a younger brother to take care of and a street gang that's looking to me for leadership. Marcus's idea is a good one.

Still, there are drawbacks to consider. "You know if we do this, we're going to have a target on our backs until this is carried through. I'm not saying that you're wrong, just that if we go through with it, he's not going to stop. We're going to need to go fast and brutal. Like Caesar crossing the fucking Rubicon. Once we do it, there ain't no going back."

Marcus shrugs. He was a little younger when Pop was gunned down. For him, the pain isn't any more or less, but it is more visceral, more in the gut. "You know me, Ryker. I'm fine with that. I've been willing to die for this chance for five years now. Besides, he won't do shit if we have his precious wife."

Precious wife. What an understatement. Sarah Waters is Jacob's prized possession. I've met her before, something I don't think anyone else knows except for maybe Marcus.

Back before she met Jacob, she was known as Sarah Desjardins, or just Sarah D. if you were more into pop culture. She'd done some teen shows, the sort of angsty teen shit that I wasn't into even when I was that age, but she certainly made watching that chick flick shit easier. She always had that elegance, that sort of innocence combined with a physical maturity that looked beyond her years. I know that her show where she spent at least half of each episode in a Catholic school-girl uniform was popular with guys, mostly for the

7

spank bank material she provided an entire generation of guys my age.

Then Sarah D. found out that being a teen hottie doesn't always translate to success past the age of twenty-one. That's when I met her, although she probably doesn't remember. She'd come into the city to do some B-grade action flick that was trying to pretend it was A-list. I worked security for fun, helping a guy Pop knew, and Pop knew I liked movies. One day, I'd even been given the task of escorting Miss Sarah D. from makeup to the set, keeping the fans she had off her.

There had been one guy, one of those pervy types I'd come to spot a mile away even with my inexperience, a little too old to be looking for an autograph for himself and a little too young to be looking for autographs for his kids. That and the way his eyes had a sort of desperate shine to them. When he made a move toward her, I very calmly grabbed his wrist and twisted it behind his back, throwing him onto the sidewalk face first.

"Thanks," Sarah told me, giving me an appreciative glance. I think it was the first time she really saw me, and at the time, I felt like there was some kind of connection. She even reached out, putting a hand on my shoulder when there was a little bit of privacy, and I could see she wanted to say something, except some assistant yelled for her on set. "See you later," she'd told me. "Let's talk some time."

But I never got a chance. That asshole obsessed fan

complained and got me reassigned to a different part of the set, and I wasn't around her as much after that. Something about liability risk.

She doesn't remember me for damn sure, but it was that same movie where she met Jacob Waters. The tabloids had a field day during their six-month whirlwind courtship, considering that his second wife had just disappeared a year before, but even then, Waters didn't give a fuck. He was dating a woman who was named one of *Young Hollywood's Top Twenty-Five Hottest Under Twenty-Five*, a woman younger than half his age. They got married, and a month later, my Pop was dead.

Since then, Waters keeps Sarah like some people keep a piece of jewelry. He parades her around on his arm, his grin always seeming to say *I've got it all, and you don't*. There isn't a society event in the city where she's not beside him looking like a million bucks. Even now, five years into the marriage, although she's officially retired from Hollywood, she gets headlines. It's easy to see why. She's beautiful. Long, black hair that hangs nearly to her waist, a light natural tan to her skin that is supposedly the result of a little bit of Gypsy blood to go with her French maiden name in her background, and a sensuality that certainly adds to that rumor.

But on the other hand, like a well-kept poodle, she's spoiled. She doesn't go anywhere without either Jacob or a couple of bodyguards. Or both. Prada and Gucci are to her what Hanes and Levis are to me.

Still, that body, those dark, mysterious eyes, and even

the fact that she's tall for a woman, just a shade under six feet . . . I can't help but crave her. I have ever since I was a teen myself. And there were those few minutes, no matter how hard I try to get them out of my head, that still make me muse, *what if?*

Not that it matters. Marcus is right. Either Sarah Waters is as corrupt as her husband, a gold digger who doesn't care that the gold is above and beyond blood-stained, or she's so fucking stupid that taking her out of the world might just do humanity a favor. But I refuse to believe the last part. With her in our posses-sion, we can cripple Jacob Waters just long enough to destroy the rest of his castle and make it crumble down around him.

"If we're going to get Sarah Waters, we need a distrac-tion. We do that, and we distract Jacob. We'll start with his crew, his friends. Who are the fuck-faces who are closest to him?"

"Sal Francisco for sure, but also Jimmy Carlson and Julio Gonzales," Marcus says right off the bat. "Why? What are you thinking?"

I turn, looking back out at the lights of the city, the speckled chaos of the city helping me think. "Those three—they get together on a regular basis, playing poker, if I remember right. We take out those three all at once, and it'll get Jacob's attention and send the sort of message that we want to send. Get with our boys who have ears and info. I want to know when and where those three are playing together again. We go in, and we hit them hard."

Marcus nods. "I'll get right on it."

"Also, find two men with steady hands, good ones to back us up," I reply, taking my hands out of my pockets and clasping them behind my back. "You have to figure that they'll have men with them, let's say six on four, with us having the element of surprise. So, I want their deaths to be . . . noticeable. Something that'll get Jacob and his pretty, pampered wife out of his mansion in order to attend the funeral. See to it."

Marcus turns and leaves, leaving me alone, looking out on the streets, watching as the lights move and the blood flows. Soon now, it'll run red with blood.

Every time the king dies, there's always a little bloodshed.

CHAPTER 2

*T*he room is just a little chilly, but at least after my shower, it helps me to remember that I'm real. It's not pain. It's more like dipping my body in a cool stream to help me wake up. Except that I'm not sleepy, and the dream isn't a dream. It's a nightmare.

"Mrs. Waters, Mr. Jacob told me that you're supposed to wear this," Constanza, the maid, says. I'm naked from the waist up, my towel wrapped around my waist for convenience's sake only, looking at the body that at one time had men drooling over me, saying nothing to Stanzie as I look at my breasts. They'd once been called 'the two greatest pieces of evidence that God is a man." I doubt that the horny editor who penned that line to go along with my photo spread for that magazine would think of them that way now. Not with the scars that dot them or the deeper ones that cover my back.

I don't hide my body here at home. Stanzie knows

about my scars. They all know that my 'loving husband' beats me. They know that the big pucker-shaped star a little over my right nipple is from a cigar that he put out on my skin. They know about the longer ones where he's beaten me with his belt. Dozens of scars. And not a single stitch in five years.

I don't blame Stanzie, though. She's just as terrified of Jacob as I am. An illegal immigrant who came to the city from Brazil on the promise of becoming an au pair, she lasted a week before Jacob raped her in front of me while I lay tied up and beaten half-senseless on the bed. She's just as terrified of him as I am. Probably even more.

They all are.

Which is why none of them are willing to help me.

Instead, I continue to brush out my hair, one of the few things that Jacob hasn't cut or abused since we got married. He likes it long, and despite all the other abuse I've received, my hair is still just as thick and strong as ever. I wish it would go brittle and break off more easily when he grabs it and drags me through the marble hallways of his mansion, but it doesn't. I hate it, while at the same time, I take a little bit of perverse pride in it. At least from the neck up, I'm still the Sarah D. who used to make men's knees weak. I'm still the girl who grew up in the suburbs and thought she had a bright future ahead of her, a girl with humor and happiness. At least it's somewhere inside me. It would be nice to pretend I'm still that girl, but at least I have my memories. Although lately, they're slipping.

"Mrs. Waters?" Stanzie says again softly. "Are you okay?"

I set my brush down, nodding. "Yes, Stanzie. Would you help me, please? My back's a bit stiff after yesterday's workout."

Workout. Stanzie doesn't say anything about my obvious lie. She knows it's because of Jacob but lets me get away with it.

Instead, she goes over to my dresser, taking out the Agent Provocateur lingerie that Jacob insists I wear. He picks out everything for me, all of it being sexy and just walking the line toward slutty, AP lingerie and form-fitting dresses that are just a little too tight or a little too revealing so that I look the part of the gold-digger tramp who's fucking her way to her inheritance. I know better than to question him or to try to be anything different. I learned that long ago.

I slide on the thong panties that Stanzie has set out. I feel for her, but considering the number of times Jacob has screamed at her that he's only treating her like garbage because of me, she might hate me just as much as she hates Jacob. Hates him and fears him.

Next is my bra, which thankfully, because of my scars, is more comfortable, with wider shoulder straps and padded, lined cups that make my breasts seem bigger to a casual observer. Jacob likes it when I look curvier when we go out. It hides the scars though. He's careful to make sure that anything he does to me can be hidden to keep up appearances.

I don't hear him. He can move like a goddamned cat when he wants to, but Stanzie and I both can feel his presence the moment he walks into my room. It was that presence that I was at first attracted to. I thought it was charisma, wit, and that quality that some people like to call 'Alpha male-ness'. I was drawn to that power. Of course, he'd been charming then, too. He's a good liar, and it wasn't until it was too late that I realized just how much of a monster he really is.

Stanzie stiffens, and even my fingers tighten a little before she can hand me the cocktail dress that I'm supposed to wear this evening for our event at the Philharmonic.

"Constanza. Out," Jacob says, and she disappears like a ghost, without even giving me a glance of pity. It's probably better for her that way.

I stand stock-still, frozen in place like a marble statue as my husband of five years, Jacob Waters, comes closer. I'm tall, but he's still taller. He's already dressed in his suit pants and shirt, although it looks like he hasn't gotten his tie on yet.

"You certainly do look seductive tonight," Jacob says, running a finger up my arm and over my shoulder. Coldness pricks my skin where he touches me, and I can't help it. He starts walking a hand up my back as he draws closer and closer to the mark that truly broke me, and I shiver. I don't think it's fear. I don't feel fear anymore. I *wish* I did. It's just physical disgust.

"This one is so beautiful," he whispers gleefully, tracing the deep fold in my skin. Belt buckles can do so much. "A harsh lesson, but you learned from it, more or less."

More or less? Yeah, I guess I did learn my lesson. It was the time that I learned that trying to run from Jacob Waters was useless. It was the time I realized just how much of a monster he is and that the cops in this town are in his pocket. I'd gone to them after watching Jacob kill a man by throwing him off the balcony of his office building.

Not that it helped. The cops handcuffed me and brought me back to the mansion, dropping me off in the foyer and leaving the cuffs on before shaking hands with Jacob and leaving me to his *lesson*. So yeah, I did learn my lesson. If I'm ever going to escape, I'm going to have to kill this man.

Jacob grabs the back of my head and my throat, painfully twisting my head to the side to look him in his icy blue eyes that burn with gleeful madness. "Ooh, Baby was thinking naughty things."

"No—" I start to reply, but Jacob doesn't care. There's no use. Pain shoots up and down my spine as he shakes me a few times by my neck, his face twisting into a mask of insane joy.

"Oh, yes, you were. I know what you're thinking. I

know exactly what you're thinking every moment of every day. And you were thinking very bad things about your Daddy, weren't you?"

His hand loosens a little on my throat, allowing me to take a breath that feels like pure moonshine being poured down my throat, and I sob. I can't help it and I hate showing weakness, but the shame in the decision I made to get with him reduces me to crying again as Jacob eyes me carefully. Finally, he half drags me across the room toward my bed, shoving me back onto the bed as he reaches for his belt, undoing it but mercifully leaving it in the belt loops.

"Oh, yes, you were naughty, and Daddy's going to have to punish you," Jacob rasps, his voice rising until it's almost girlish, a far cry from the deep, powerful tones that the public knows him for. "Daddy's going to have to punish you good."

I start to cry. What's worse, and what adds to my shame, is that my mind tells me that this is what I get. Everyone told me not to get involved with him, that he was trouble, from day one. This hell is all I get to look forward to for the rest of my miserable life until I find a way to kill him. If that day ever comes.

Jacob doesn't take it further though. He's content that he's made his point, and I'm sobbing in shame when I feel temporarily relieved. "Oh, be quiet. I'll leave you alone. I'll send Constanza in to help you get ready for the night out. But just remember, I own you."

He leaves, and in the temporary silence, I want to scream into my pillow in rage and helplessness, but my screams are silent. I know better than to disobey him.

It's a death wish, but I can't wait until I have the perfect opportunity to put him six feet under. I'll go to Hell a happy woman if I can send him there just a few seconds before me.

CHAPTER 3

"*A*re you ready, Ryker?" Marcus asks, and I'm grateful again for my brother. While he may think he's just doing things anyone could do, it's at times like this that I most appreciate his presence. I feel the weight of the potential deaths on my mind. Not of the three assholes we're aiming for, but of Marcus, Javier, and Eric, the two hitters Marcus chose to help us with this job.

Marcus isn't like me in that regard. Sure, he knows Javy and Eric better than I do—that's his job. He knows the boys. I need that sort of distance from them because deep down, I care about them too much to want to risk them. It's hard enough risking my brother. Myself . . . well, that's just the way it goes.

His question helps me focus on the challenge at hand. Tonight's poker game is happening at The Lucky Seven Tavern, where there's a very lucrative underground casino in the back room. Where money isn't the only thing thrown into the pot during the game, but rather things that you can't exactly exchange in the casino a hundred miles down the road. Six men—the three targets plus three more men who are unimportant to me except as potential guns—and a few bodyguards.

"Yeah, I'm ready," I finally reply, going over to the scratched desk in the warehouse we're using as a staging area for tonight's attack and picking up the Saiga-12 that I'm using for tonight's hit. Marcus is carrying the same thing. Two semiautomatic shotguns are enough for this, while Javy and Eric will be carrying MP-5s. It's one of the first lessons I learned when I started bringing the gangs together, one I borrowed from the military as I took my brains from studying at a community college and applied them to running this thing. Everyone showing up with whatever Saturday Night Special they wanted to bring to the party is a good way to find yourself fucked up very quickly. Good troops need good equipment, so I've made sure that my men carry the best we can get our hands on.

That lesson becomes clear when I see Javier holding not the MP-5 that I ordered, but an Uzi in his hands when I come out of the office, making me stop. "What the fuck is that?"

He's a new kid, a steady hand so far, and he's proven to be loyal and eager to make something of himself. But he's from the South Side, which for a long time was disrespected around town. I don't believe in it, but some still do. I can read in Javy's eyes that he wants to make an impression tonight. "It's my baby. I call her Charlene."

I roll my eyes, holding up a hand when Marcus takes a step forward. I'll handle this. "Put the bitch away. That's not what we're here for."

"Why?" Javier asks, a trifle unsure but not wanting to come off as a punk. Little does he know that by standing up to me, he's just making it worse for himself. "Charlene can pump lead just as good as those German death machines."

I step closer and take the Uzi from him. Without warning, I turn and spray the Uzi across the other end of the warehouse. We're secluded enough that the sound won't be noticed. "Now that you're out of ammo, what the fuck good are you?"

"But . . ." Javy says as I hand the now empty Uzi back to him. "I mean—"

"This isn't some goddamned Stallone movie where our guns have magic magazines that never run out of rounds," I interrupt, grabbing him by the collar of his shirt and jamming the gun into his chest. "And you don't have any spare mags for your gun! What are you going to do, tell everyone to stop while you hand-load spare rounds, one by one, into your mag? Put Charlene down."

Javier's stunned, but he does as he's told. Eric, who's

23

been with us from the beginning, just chuckles and follows behind, climbing in the back and closing the door. Marcus gives me a chagrined look. "Sorry, Ryker. Thought he would've known better than that."

"He's young. He'll learn. As long as he's a good hand in the fight, I'm not worried about him being a bit cocky. Come on."

We climb into the van, and I see that Eric's already climbed behind the driver's seat, leaving shotgun for Marcus and the back for Javy and me. The engine starts up, and we pull out, Javier and I looking at each other across the back of the van.

"Mr. Ryker?" Javier finally says to break the silence. He sounds different this time. Maybe he's ready to actually learn. "Why'd you do that, anyway?"

"The people we're going to hit tonight, they've been able to keep us down for years because they've treated us like doormats. We have the numbers, my friend. For every cop, for every 'made man' in the mobs who looks down on us, there's four street-level soldiers. We should have had this city a long damn time ago. But we helped them, we let them divide us, put us against each other over stupid shit like what color our skin is or what street we represent. They thought we were incapable of coming together, and the fact is, we weren't for a long time. That shit stops. We work together, we cooperate, and we can take this city."

"You mean *you* take the city," Javier says, and I shrug.

"Every unit has to have a leader. At least I still remember what it was like looking forward to my state paid-for lunch at school and my cheap shit government beans and cheese dinner. I haven't forgotten the hustle. And I haven't forgotten how to get my hands dirty. Like tonight."

Javier nods, looking at his MP-5. I can tell he's thinking. He's had a life like mine. Maybe the foods were different, but he understands. Finally, he looks up. "Okay then. My bad about Charlene."

I offer my hand, and we shake before we sit back. The staging area was a good way from The Lucky Seven, and it takes us a while. Finally, Marcus speaks up from the front. "There it is, Ryker."

I scoot forward, looking out the front window as I see The Lucky Seven Tavern. The sign is practically a fucking advertisement for what goes on in the back, a pair of dice showing a four and a three superimposed over a martini glass, but the cops don't give a fuck as long as they get their kickbacks. They play their games and we play ours.

"Okay, pull up to the side entrance down the alley. That's where the casino door is," I say. I take a second and look around at the others. "Remember the plan. Hit them hard and fast. No casualties other than the three fucksticks we're after and any bodyguards. We clear?"

Everyone nods, and Eric pulls the van up in front of the casino door. "GO!"

I know there's a security camera, so we don't have much time as we throw open the sliding door on the driver's side, Eric and Javy getting out first. Marcus has the slowest route, having to come around. "Down!"

The Saiga roars, the twelve-gauge deer slug hitting the door near the locks and punching a hole through. Steel-core doors aren't shit for a slug fired from eighteen inches away. With a kick of my boot, the door flies open, and I fire again into whatever the fuck's in the way.

Javy's first, his ego and *machismo* making him break discipline, and he pays for it, the shot from the bodyguard inside taking him high in the left shoulder. It doesn't matter. My shotgun makes quick work of the shooter a half second later while Eric's already doing his job, spraying the poker table in front of us with an entire forty-round clip while Marcus and I shove through the door. Marcus once again shows his guts as he steps in front of the sagging Javier to protect him.

Somehow, miraculously, Sal Francisco is still alive, his hands over his head, pressed down against the table after Eric's sweep with his gun, and I take him out first, blowing him out of his chair. Julio Gonzales is on the floor, but Jimmy's up, his reflexes a lot faster than a man his age normally has. My next shot takes him in the hip, destroying his ability to walk while spinning him to the floor and adding his screams to the overall insanity. He's neutralized, and I fire again, putting him down. "Hold!"

Eric takes a little longer than the others, finishing out his current magazine before he stops, and we survey the damage. The table, which at one point looked like it might have been dark oak covered in green felt, looks like firewood with green puffs of fuzz on top, and the metal chairs have been twisted into strange, fantastical shapes as rounds have blasted them into scrap. The stench of burned gunpowder overpowers everything, although the coppery smell of blood is already starting to undercut it and make its presence felt.

Through the wall, I can hear a little bit of reaction from the patrons of the Lucky Seven. The walls are sound-proofed but not that well. Miraculously, I can hear a woman's whimpers, and crouched down in the corner is a girl who was obviously here for entertainment purposes after the poker was finished, if her Playboy Bunny outfit is to mean anything. She's covered in a mist of blood, we all are, and when I go over to nudge her with the toe of my boot, she screams, looking up at me with bright green eyes. "Please! Please don't kill me!"

"I'm not going to hurt you," I reply softly, squatting down. Eric's already pulling back, pulling the injured Javier with him while Marcus covers me, making sure there's nobody playing possum. "I need you to deliver a message to someone for me, though."

"Who?" the girl asks, her voice like a little girl's from

the shock. Not what I intended, but at least she's uninjured.

"Tell them . . . this town is Ryker's," I say softly, standing up and shouldering my Saiga. "Tell them that if they don't know that now, they'll find out soon enough."

The girl nods, and I turn, casually walking out the door.

I turn my attention to Javier, who's panicked and in shock from the gunshot. Luckily for him, I prepared for this. "Chill, Javy. The doctor's just a few miles away. He'll get you fixed up. He's the best around. In the meantime, just chill, lie back, and think of the stories you'll get to tell about this. Besides, chicks dig scars."

Javier tries to smile, but it hurts, so he just grimaces and nods. "Sorry, Ryker."

"No sweat, man. We're gonna get you stitched up, you'll rest up a little, and then you'll be back in no time. You showed guts, which is number one. We'll work on getting those guts under control later."

Nobody says anything else until we get to the doctor's place, dropping Eric and Javier off at the underground clinic while Marcus and I head off to ditch the van. As I drive, Marcus rides shotgun, his eyes constantly sweeping the streets around us. "So, Ryker, about Doc . . ."

"Yeah?" I ask, and Marcus looks over.

"You do know that he's not a real doctor, right? He was just a Navy Corpsman who went to State on an ROTC scholarship."

I nod, giving my brother a smirk. "I know that. You know that. But Javier doesn't need to know. He'll be fine. Now, on to business. After tonight, we've got to be ready to move and move fast. The next hit's going to be at the funeral for Sal Francisco. If we're lucky, we might even get a shot in on Jacob Waters himself."

Marcus nods, his hands tightening on the steering wheel. "We'll be ready."

CHAPTER 4

*B*reakfast is light, which I'm glad for. After getting the news that Sal Francisco was killed along with some other men in his group, Jacob's been on edge. I'm eager to finish and stay out of his sight. Stanzie, on the other hand, hasn't been as lucky as me. Her left eye is half-closed from the slap he gave her last night when she supposedly looked at him wrong. I should feel bad for her, but I don't. I know it's wrong, I really do, but I'm practically numb to what Jacob does to us now.

The only good thing is that he's been busy. The hit was messy, according to what the men who've come to the mansion have said. They gossip almost constantly whenever they get a chance, filling the time they're standing around with bragging and gossiping. They're worse than old women that way. There's a name they keep saying too . . . Ryker. It's a name I've heard more and more over the past few months. Apparently, he's some sort of street gang leader. They say that he and three of his boys hit the card game that Sal Francisco, Jimmie Clausen, and Julio Gonzales were playing at. From the way they're talking, Ryker took out at least two of the three men himself. Until the hit on the game, Jacob talked about Ryker like someone would talk about a particularly annoying fly. Not anymore.

"I said after the funeral, I want the best men in town to hunt that motherfucker down and bring me his balls in a silver bowl!" Jacob yells into his phone. He's pacing back and forth, running his free hand through his silvery gray hair, looking like neither the distinguished tough, bargaining real estate tycoon the law-abiding public knows, nor the badass mob boss the other side of society knows. Instead, he looks like he's just this side of unhinged, and a lot older too. "I don't care if it gets messy! I don't care if he's got every street rat from the South Side to the Tracks to the Narrows on his side. I want him dead!"

I cringe and quickly go to my room, seeing that I've got about ninety minutes before we need to leave for the funeral. Stanzie joins me soon, but I wave her away. The poor woman has been through enough. She should do like me and stay hidden. "Go rest, Stanzie. Is the house clean?"

"Yes, Mrs. Waters," she says, her voice quavering. "Thank you."

Watching her leave breaks my heart. She's grateful for

even this little bit of reprieve, and the first inevitable dark thoughts start to fill my head. Stanzie's still fighting, but she's only been around a little while. I wonder how much fight's going to be left when she's been here as long as I have.

There's no escape. I know that, and soon, she will too.

He's done it before. He showed me what he did to his second wife, the one who supposedly disappeared while the two of them were scuba diving in Thailand. They never did find the body.

So what, exactly, is stopping me? Is it just that I hate him that much?

But hating Jacob is a lot like hating a hurricane. You can hate on it all you want, but there isn't a hell of a lot you can do to stop it from tearing the roof off your house if it wants to. All you can do is try and get out of the way, and I'm in a situation where I'm not even able to do that.

I start to get dressed, thoughts as dark as my dress swirling around my head, and I'm so deep in thought that when Jacob puts his hand on my shoulder, I'm lucky that I don't screw up my lipstick.

"You surprised me," I say softly, putting the lipstick away. "I was thinking about the funeral."

"I can see that," Jacob says, looking at me in the mirror. He doesn't say anything yet, but I can see from the look on his face that he doesn't approve. Nothing new there.

I look at myself in the mirror, and I don't think I look bad at all. Sure, the lipstick isn't deep maroon or something, but it's not like I'm wearing fire-engine red or bubblegum pink. "I just wanted to look pretty today."

Jacob glares at me in the mirror. "Show some respect. You need to be in mourning. Sal Francisco was more valuable to me than you ever were or ever will be. At least he knew how to be loyal, how to do what his betters demanded. Although . . ."

Jacob grabs me and kisses me hard, smearing my lipstick all around my face and ruining everything. When he pulls back, he laughs. "Now, maybe you'll do it right this time."

His words should sting. I should be upset. I should be wanting to cry, but for some reason, I just can't.

Five years, four months, and seventeen days is all it took to burn every bit out of me, I guess. He started our wedding night. That was when he 'got rough' for the first time, as he called it, and since then, I've had it all burned out of me, all of my self-image, all of my pride. I'm just an empty puppet doing what I'm told to do. I've got nothing left.

Instead of protesting, I look in the mirror, where I can see both of us as Jacob continues his disapproving look. Finally, I look at him directly in his cold, dead eyes. "I'll be in mourning," I say.

*H*is grimace disappears into a bit of a smile. "Good girl. Well then, I'll let you finish getting ready. We leave in twenty minutes. Meet me in the foyer."

He leaves, and I look at my face in the mirror, reaching for the towel next to my makeup kit with robotic arms, not feeling anything at all as I wipe all traces of makeup off my cheeks and mouth before carefully reapplying it. I use a different tone from before, more conservative, more subdued, with nothing for my cheeks at all. I still look beautiful, but I also look like I'm in mourning.

I guess I am, but not for the reason Jacob wants me to be. I'm mourning the woman I *could* have been. I don't want to sound too much like Brando, but I could have been somebody. I could have made the transition to legit actress. I had the skills even if I wasn't going to win any Academy Awards. Even if the typecasting had been too much, I didn't deserve this. I didn't deserve five years of abuse. I should have had a *loving* husband. I could have started a family already. I didn't deserve this.

I use eighteen of my twenty minutes to try and find a reason to work up tears on the way to the funeral, but I can't. I can be in mourning. I'm still a decent enough actress to do that, but it's going to have to be the 'stunned yet stony-faced mourner' bit. Works enough when you don't know the man being buried beyond his being one of your husband's business associates and an occasional poker buddy.

We get in the limo to ride to the church and after that, the cemetery. We're about a third of the way there when Jacob looks over, evaluating my face. "Good girl."

"Thank you," I whisper, trying to do anything I can to avoid looking at him. "I also have a hat with a veil."

"Good girl," Jacob repeats, and I can see a grin form on his face out of the corner of my eyes. A queasy feeling forms in the pit of my stomach. No, dear God, no. We're on our way to a church.

"Jacob . . .?"

He shakes his head, unbuttoning his coat and undoing his belt. "You know what to do."

Sadly, after all these years, I do. I get on my knees. I don't protest. I just shut off my mind, knowing that if I'm not already in hell, I'm just this side of it. Thankfully, it doesn't take long, and as I do everything I can to work up enough spit to get his taste out of my mouth, he speaks softly, almost gently to me. "That's it, baby. See? You listen and things go well."

a different warehouse and a different time of day, but the idea's the same. I look out at the assembled group, this time a crew of ten. The danger levels are off the charts right now, but there's a reason that Marcus and I picked these men to come with us. Every one of them has a personal reason to hate Jacob Waters but is also professional enough to do their job without fucking around on a personal vendetta.

"Remember, the idea is to cause carnage," I brief, pointing to the chalkboard where I've drawn a diagram of the action. Again, another lesson I learned from studying successful armies. Brief your soldiers. Let them understand the mission, and then when the shit hits the fan, they'll be better prepared to react to unexpected circumstances. Everyone has a role, and they need to know it. "Thankfully, the weather gods are in our favor," I continue. "They're calling for rain this afternoon, so long trench coats aren't going to look out of place."

"Damn shame to be ruining a suit like this in one day. I look like a million bucks," someone quips, earning a few laughs. I shrug. While I've got better suits, I understand. I made sure that everyone had a suit that would let them walk into any bank and look right at home, with good labels. Spending an extra couple of hundred dollars on suits is worth it if today's mission works.

"Yeah, well, I'll buy you a spare if you want it," I reply, not wanting to add the morbid thought that I may be doing that anyway, for their own funerals. "Now, everyone, let me be very, very clear. Nobody is to take a shot at Jacob Waters. Today's idea is to hit another of his lieutenants and to snatch his wife."

"Why not just put one in his head?" one of the guys asks, and I sit down on the table, relaxing. Marcus doesn't look happy about it, but that's okay. We've got a little bit of time.

"If we just cut the head off the beast, the remaining lieutenants are going to be strong enough to try and fight us. Hell, he's still popular with the police. What do you think's going to happen to our neighborhoods if the cops go rampant citywide because we shot one of their most popular crooks? No, we must remove his support, peel each group from him, and make his underlings recognize that he's not strong enough to protect them anymore. We make them realize that the real power lies with us so that when we do take him down, he's going to be friendless."

"Now, let me wrap things up," I say, glancing at my watch. There's still time, but I can see that Marcus is getting antsy. Better to keep him calm until it's time. "The target that has to be taken down is this guy, Soo-Young Pak. He's the connection Waters has with the Asian gangs overseas, so if we take him out, we take away his overseas drug and money operations. That leaves the wife, Sarah Waters. She's mine, plain and simple. Nobody touches her. I'll snag her. Is everyone clear?"

Nobody says anything, and I turn the rest of the briefing over to Marcus, pretending that I have to go take a piss. The reality is that I've got to get my head right. Last night, after Marcus had gone to bed, for some reason, I'd pulled up an old episode of Sarah's television show. I can't seem to wrap my ahead around the fact that the girl I was so fucking into back then was a fictional character, not the real-life woman who got my father killed. Even worse, I have a problem separating her from the woman I met that one bright, sunny day, the one who'd looked at me with deep, sultry eyes and thanked me. That woman, who turned out to be a snake in the grass. Still, as I shake off and tuck myself back into my suit pants, I can't get that old fantasy of fucking her in that schoolgirl outfit out of my head.

I come out, looking over the group. "Okay, any last

comments, concerns, gripes, or bitches? Now's the time."

There are no more questions, so we split up, five vehicles this time, ranging from a pickup truck to the Caddy that Marcus and I are taking. As soon as we roll up the door on the warehouse, I see that the rain's starting already, and by the color of the clouds, it's just going to get worse. "Well, well, that'll make things even easier."

"It'll be hard for folks to not want to take a shot at Waters," Marcus warns me. "Is that why you went with pistols?"

"That and hiding a shotgun under a suit coat is really fucking hard," I reply with a chuckle. "But I do want that fucker to die by my hand."

When we get to the graveyard, I put on a dark, wide-brimmed fedora to match my coat and to keep the rain out of my eyes while Marcus peels off to approach the gravesite from another direction. We're just in time as the main procession arrives minutes later and the first problem shows up. I'd expected there to be about ten cars in the burial party, but there are nearly twenty-five, which means a lot more people at the graveside. Getting close is going to be difficult.

As the crowd emerges, I see Jacob Waters getting out of a stretch limo, a better ride than even the deputy mayor, who at least had the humility to drive his own car to the graveyard. They follow behind the casket, which is carried in the old-fashioned way on the shoulders of six men who struggle a little in the now wet, slick grass.

I see my guys start to blend into the crowd, and I'm reassured when I see two of them get close to Pak. They'll have the drop on him. But I have a problem with my position. Waters is being more careful than I thought he'd be. In addition to his wife and himself, he's got a small entourage with him, three guys who are more muscle than brains, but they form a human wall behind Waters as everyone gathers around the gravesite for the final service.

The priest, his vestments already soaked from the rain despite someone trying to help him by holding an umbrella over his head, starts his speech, his voice carrying over the sound of the rain hitting the casket in an almost machine gun-like rattle. The sound is annoying, Sal Francisco was a millionaire. Why the hell he decided to get buried in a cheap, shitty, hollow aluminum casket is beyond me.

If I can't get right behind Sarah Waters, then I'm forced to move. I put myself between them and the limo, as close as I can dare without drawing attention. Then, all I can do is wait for the signal, which comes from the priest himself.

"Ashes to ashes—" he says, and a pistol shot rips through the rain, Soo-Young Pak jerking as the first shot takes him down. Screams and pistol shots fill the air, with people diving for cover. Jacob Waters's bodyguards form a human shield around him, and I make my move, expecting Sarah to head toward the car, but instead, she runs the opposite direction, surprising me.

The grass is slippery, and I need to shove three people out of the way before I see her. She's most of the way up the rise that dominates the side of the graveyard and gives it the name Forest Hill before I'm clear. I have to trust that Marcus is organizing the rest of the action while I chase Sarah up the hill, wishing I could have worn something with more tread than dress shoes as I slip, my knee sliding in the mud. I've got my own pistol, but I don't want to draw it unless I must.

We enter the trees that provide the other half of Forest Hill's name, and Sarah's running hard like she's running for her life. I think about calling out her name for an instant, but I don't, running harder. The fact is, she's long-legged, and while she might be in heels, she's on her toes and sprinting, her own coat billowing out behind her as she loses her hat and makes a turn around a tree.

She glances back, seeing me, her eyes going wide, but it's a mistake as she doesn't see the tree branch in front of her that catches her on the side of her head, knocking her to the ground. I close the gap, grabbing her just as she struggles to her feet, wrapping my arms around her from behind.

"No! Let me go!" she yells, twisting like a wet cat in my arms. "Let me go!"

"I don't think so," I growl, slipping my arm around her neck, feeling her body writhe against me. I hate that I'm doing this, but it's necessary, and I'm still careful not to hurt her.

I'm not one to engage in violence against women—that's part of my own personal code of honor—but this is for her own good, and I choke her out quickly, waiting until she's unconscious to pull the syringe from my coat pocket and inject her with enough ketamine to keep her down for a good half hour. She'll have a sore spot on her ass for a few days, but at least she'll be alive. Ketamine doesn't fuck with your breathing or heartbeat.

I sling Sarah over my shoulder and head over the hill, looking around to see if anyone's following us. I reach for the earpiece that I put in for just this sort of clusterfuck. "Marcus, I need a pickup."

"Where?" he says as I emerge from the forest, seeing the north entrance to Forest Hill in the distance.

"On the north-side road, closest to the hill. Hurry."

"One minute," Marcus says, and I squat down, making sure to stay in the shadows. It's actually a minute and ten seconds by my count when Marcus comes around the corner, and I rush down the hill, slamming the trunk closed on Sarah Waters's knocked-out form before jumping in the back of the car. Marcus peels out, not slowing down until we're a half-mile away and we're approaching the freeway.

"What's the count?" I ask, untying the belt on my coat. I don't really want to know, but I need to.

Marcus knows exactly what I mean. "Two of our guys down, one wounded. We got our main target. Also . . ."

"Yeah?" I ask, worried that Marcus is about to say that an innocent bystander got shot.

"Jacob Waters is going to be walking with a limp," Marcus says, looking up into the rearview mirror with a grin. "I put a round right in his ass."

I can't help it, I laugh. "Okay then. Let's get to the house, and we can discuss what to do after we get a hot shower and some fresh clothes. That rain was icy."

CHAPTER 6

The first thing I feel when I come to is a bump, and my left knee hits something hard. I yelp in pain, but I don't think anyone can hear me. I can't sense that anyone is near me.

It takes me a minute to realize where I am—the trunk of a car. I can hear the sound of the pavement whizzing underneath me, the sound of the engine up front, and the occasional sound of some piece of road dirt pinging off the bottom of the car.

Whoever it was that took me, I suspect that they don't work for Jacob. It's not particularly his style of sadism. If it were he who had me, I'd be treated like a princess until he could get his hands on me for running. So whoever has me, they've got their own agenda. And from what I know, no one has ever attacked him like this before.

It's strange that as I shift around to get my hip away from the warm spot that the exhaust pipe's causing, I feel something inside me waking up after a long sleep. When the shooting started at the funeral and Jacob's bodyguards collapsed on him, I don't know why I reacted the way I did. Maybe I'm not as willing to die as I thought, because instead of just standing there or following Jacob, I used the momentary distraction to run the opposite direction, up the hill and into the trees.

I'd thought that the man who chased me was just another of my husband's men, that he had four men instead of three. And amazingly, I felt fear. It was tangy and delicious in my mouth as I ran in a panic, although it also led to my being stupid and looking back.

Still, for the rest of the ride, I lay on my side quietly, savoring the flavor of my fear. I thought that everything inside me was dead, but now, there's something still kicking inside Sarah Desjardins that might still want to live a little bit longer. I turn it around and around in my brain, wondering if there's a chance that it'll spark the rest of me into wanting to live, but I'm so tired, and whatever they used to knock me out is still throwing me for a loop. I think I was injected. I've got a sore spot on my right ass cheek that reminds me of when I had to get a rabies vaccination after an animal on set bit me when I was thirteen.

We keep going for I don't know how long. Time feels weird when you're locked in a trunk. Eventually, the car stops. I can hear the echo of an enclosed space, and the engine stops.

Fresh fear strikes me as I hear two doors open and then shut, and two sets of footsteps approach the back of the trunk. "So, how do you want to do it?"

"Let's see if she's willing to be cooperative," the other voice says, and I hear the clicking sound of a key being put in the trunk's lock. Suddenly, I'm staring up into bright fluorescents. I squint, trying to see my captors, but I can't see anything except dark blobs against a bright white background. "Shit, I didn't see that before."

"What?" the second voice says, and I feel something cold press against my ankle before there's a snipping sound, and I realize what they saw. I've worn my tracker anklet for so long that I barely even feel it anymore.

"Take this and throw it in the river," the one says, and I can't make him out very well. My eyes are still dazzled by the sudden brightness after the darkness of the trunk. "It's got a tracker chip in it."

"Gotcha. Is it dangerous?" the other asks, and I can hear in the voices that they're related somehow. Their speech is pretty similar, not just in tone but in cadence, in pattern. Another side effect of learning acting is voice recognition.

"No, I don't think so. Hurry, though."

The other one walks off, and I'm left to look at the one who stayed behind. I still can't see much. My eyes are still dazzled, and all I know is that he's a huge shadow against the parking lot lights. "Well, the ketamine's still got you a little rubbery-legged, so I guess you'll have to go up the old-fashioned way," he says, reaching in and grabbing me with immensely powerful hands. I'm not that big a girl, but I am nearly six feet tall, and that means that I'm no feather, yet still, he puts me over his shoulder like a sack of potatoes and closes the trunk, heading for the elevators. "Can you talk?"

"I can talk," I mumble, vowing that as soon as I get a chance, I'm going to get away from here. I never could get away from Jacob, and I'm not going to just be passed around like a bargaining chip from one abuser to the next. At least with Jacob, I knew what to expect. I have no fucking clue who these men are and I'm afraid to find out. They must be on another level of scary if they're willing to take on Jacob. "You're a dead man. He'll find me," I say, hoping to scare them I guess. "You can't hide from him."

"Oh, I totally plan on letting him know where you are," the man says in amusement, walking into the elevator. The doors close, and we go up fast. This must be some sort of an express. "Because I'm going to tell exactly where you are and who has you. I just sent Marcus to throw your anklet in the river to give us a few hours to get you situated and to get this place secured."

"I won't make it easy for you," I whisper, trying to hit his back, but either I'm weaker than I thought or he's made of granite because my fists just bang off his back without him feeling them at all. "Let me go, motherfucker!"

"You're not going anywhere, Sarah," the man says. "And if you keep hitting me in the back, I'm going to put you in an arm lock to walk you off the elevator. I'd prefer not to do that. This will be a lot easier if you just cooperate. If you do, no harm will come to you. You have my word."

So, this asshole has some sort of code of honor. I can hear it in his voice. I note that and remind myself that as soon as I get a chance, I'm going to have to use it against him to make a break for it.

The elevator stops, and we step off, my captor letting me down to stand on my own two unsteady feet. "Will you walk, or will I have to carry you inside?"

I can see his face now, and I'm surprised at just how handsome this man is. He's got that sort of face that doesn't look like it should belong to a man in the twenty-first century, with blond hair and icy blue eyes that look like he belongs in a Viking action drama, not wearing a wet trench coat and looking like he's ready for a business meeting. Still, there's profound intelligence there, intelligence and a sort of cold-bloodedness that tells me that while he might not like the idea of hurting me, he will without a second's hesitation if I make an issue of things.

"I can walk," I reply, and he takes my upper arm in a strong grip, not squeezing but still iron hard, uncompromising. Still, compared to what I've felt over the past five years, it's almost a gentle caress, and I follow him without as much fight as I thought I might at first.

We go through the main double doors to what is obviously the penthouse suite of whatever building we're in, and I'm taken aback at the unexpected luxury of the space. There are large open ceilings, and all the furniture is beautifully modern, with lots of rich, deep tones in leather, dark tiles, and metal accents. "Your boss has good taste, whoever he is," I say, fishing to see if he'll say who his boss is and not intending it to be a compliment.

"I *am* the boss. Unlike your husband, I don't mind getting down and taking ownership of my work," the blond man says. "But thank you for the compliment."

His thanks sound reasonably legitimate, and I don't know why, but my fear both ratchets up and relaxes a little at the same time. It takes me a moment to realize why, though. It's that Jacob started the same way, complimenting me before he turned into the fucking devil.

The man leads me into one of the bedrooms, where I look out and am once again impressed with the view, looking over the lake and off into the distance. "In the afternoons at sunset, you'll have some direct sunlight in your eyes, but we'll be pulling the curtain anyway."

He leads me to the dresser, where I see pieces of rope and a set of handcuffs already laid out. It causes me to struggle, but his hand is still iron-hard, and he ignores my attempts to get free as he quickly cuffs my left hand, twisting my arm behind my back and pushing me onto the bed. "No, please! Please, don't rape me!" I plead.

He pauses for a second, then I hear the other end of the handcuff click around the bedpost. "I wouldn't do that," he says, backing away. "That's the sort of sick shit your husband does. Not me."

The way he's cuffed me leaves me room to turn over and even get off the bed if I want. I lie there instead, looking at him with suspicious wonder. "You don't?"

"A real man doesn't need to force a woman," he says, disgust in his voice. "What sort of fucking monster do you think I am?"

"You kidnapped me, for one," I reply, sitting up as much as I can. "Why should I think you're any better? You've handcuffed me to a bed."

"With a handcuff that gives you room to move," he points out. He goes over to the dresser and picks up the rope. "And the only reason I'm doing this is for my protection and yours. There's no lock on the room door, so for my safety, I need to keep you in here. For your safety, the elevator's on a PIN code control, so the only way outside for you is the balcony. We're forty-eight floors up, and you're not Spiderman."

He runs the rope through his hand, then puts it back on the dresser. "I'll make you a deal. If you promise not to act a damn fool, I'll let you stay with just the handcuff. If you get up to any fuckery, though, I'll tie your ankles together and truss you up on this bed like a Christmas ham. Deal?"

I nod, shifting back to sit up. "Deal. So . . . why'd you do it? Money?"

The man laughs in genuine amusement, shaking his head. As he does, I can't help but think that he might be a cold-blooded monster like my husband, but he's got the looks of an angel. "Not that there won't be money involved eventually, but no. No, I did it because I'm going to kill your husband. I'm going to take his empire away from him, and the last thing he's going to see is my hand holding his throat and the knowledge that I've taken everything from him—his empire, his money, his position, his honor . . . and yes, even you. His debt to me and my family will finally be paid."

I think about it, then nod. Maybe he's an angel in disguise, come to grant my deepest wish. Not all angels have to carry harps, after all. "Good."

The man blinks, and I think that for the first time, I've shocked him a little. I don't give a fuck if he is. I hope he succeeds. "Good?"

I nod, my lip curling unconsciously. "Good. I wish I could give you something that would help you kill the fucker. But I don't know anything."

"I see. That surprises me a little, and sorry if I don't believe you, Sarah. But if you're telling me the truth, then I may have to move a little faster in my plan," the man says. His eyes burn with intensity, and finally, I need to look away from him, out through the floor-to-ceiling glass windows out over the lake. I'm terrified, but I'll admit that I'm also bit attracted to him, and that's dangerous. So instead, I watch the lake and the birds flying over it before I close my eyes and look back.

"Why didn't you kill him then?" I ask him, not looking him in the eyes. "You had men there. You had a shot for sure. I remember seeing your hat, thinking not too many men know how to wear a hat like that anymore. They either come off like hipster douches or kids playing dress-up."

The man goes over to a chair and takes off his trench coat, revealing a splendid suit underneath. Whoever he is, he's got style, that's for damn sure. "I didn't kill him because, like I said, I want to take everything from him. Killing the fucker is too easy. I could have done that a year ago. No, I want everything taken from him like he took everything from me. He owes me a debt."

There's something in his voice that shows me a deep-seated pain, and I twist my head, looking up at him. "What's your name?"

For the first time since opening the trunk, I know I've angered him as he gets up, undoing his coat and pulling off his tie. "You're going to pretend not to know? How the fuck can you just sit there and say you don't know who I am? You're half the fucking reason I'm where I am today!"

I don't understand what he means. "How would I know you?"

He crosses the room in what feels like the blink of an eye, reaching for my free hand to pull me up to look at him more closely. I have no idea what he's doing, so I try to fight him, but with the handcuff, I can't do anything except try to push him away with my right hand and my feet. He grabs ahold of my coat and dress, looking me right in the eye. It doesn't feel like he's trying to assault me, but out of instinct, I kick. I catch him right in the thigh with enough force to drop most men, but not him. His grip on my dress doesn't loosen at all, and my dress tears. The man takes a single stumbling step back while I go rolling off the bed, my left shoulder sending shooting pains up my arm as I twist, but I feel more alive than I have in years. I feel a fight in me that I thought Jacob had taken away. I feel like a human being again.

The man turns, his blue eyes flaring with anger before he stops, staring at me in open shock again. He raises a hand, pointing. "What . . . what are those?"

I look down, and I see that my dress is torn worse than I thought and that most of my right side is revealed, except for the part of my breast covered with my bra. Still, I'm not sure what he's talking about. I'm just pissed and scared. "It's my right breast, you fucking idiot. Is this how you normally introduce yourself to a woman? Don't tell her your name, assume she knows who the fuck you are, then rip half her dress off before asking her what a tit is?"

I can see the anger flare in his eyes for a second before something else takes over, and he shakes his head. "Not that. Under your bra strap. And in . . . in your cleavage."

I know what he's talking about, but I still look down, seeing the deeply puckered welt in my flesh, and my rage disappears as my embarrassment starts. I look up at my captor with shame in my eyes, but that new fire in my gut isn't willing to disappear just yet. "It's why I hope you end up killing that bastard who calls himself my husband. It's not all he's done."

I shrug, getting the rest of my dress off my upper body, and I turn around, showing him my back. When I turn back around, he's looking at me with an expression that nobody has used with me for five years. It hurts worse than any punch or kick that I could have expected, and I feel tears start to trickle down my face. "So, what do you think?"

He steps back, gathering himself as he goes over to his suit coat and picks it up off the carpet and heads to the door. "I think I'm doing the world a favor by killing your husband. It doesn't make me a saint, but at least I'm not a monster. By the way, the name's Ryker. Ryker Johns. Someone will be back later with some dry clothes and dinner for you. In the meantime, feel free to use the blankets, and hell, tear that dress off if you want. Welcome to my home, Sarah D."

Sarah D. Nobody's called me that in years, and as he closes the door, I wonder just what the hell is going to happen to me. I do know one thing. For the first time in a very long time, I *want* to live.

Something in Ryker's strength and in the way he spoke sparks a memory inside my head. And it dawns on me —he's the cute security guy, the one who threw that creepy bastard on his ass. I remember the day well.

I'd been in town for the movie shoot, and somewhere along the line, I'd picked up a stalkerish fan. That day, creepy bastard had somehow gotten past the outer security and was approaching me, but the security guy who'd been assigned to watch me handled him so fast that I barely had time to blink. It was only after it was over that I really noticed him and how cute he was.

We'd only exchanged a few words, but for the rest of the shoot, I sort of looked out for him and was disappointed when one of the production assistants told me he was reassigned because the company was scared that they'd get sued if he roughed up anyone again.

And now he's back in my life, and he says that he's going to kill Jacob. Could he be my savior once again?

CHAPTER 7

RYKER

*I*t's dark by the time Marcus comes back, a couple of bags of McDonald's tucked under his arm. "You sure you wanted Mickey D's, man? I mean, no offense, but you usually eat a lot better than this."

I shrug, looking out the window at the sparkling streets below, sipping at the scotch I poured myself after changing. I had to. Something about seeing Sarah hurt the way she was shakes me to my core. Nobody expects those teen sensations to be perfect once they reach adulthood, but Sarah D.—she was practically royalty to me. Even the time I worked on the movie set with her, she wasn't really a bitch. She even said thank you when I walked her to the set. And ever since leaving her in the spare bedroom, I can nearly feel the touch of her arm in my hand.

When I close my eyes, I see her body. What Jacob did

to her makes my blood boil . . . but she's still so beautiful that it takes my breath away. Her body, despite the deep scars, ignited passions inside me that I normally keep under tight control. The way her hair gleamed, the light duskiness of her skin, even her smile was still perfect in its bloodthirstiness when I said I was going to kill her husband. Even more beautiful was the fire I saw in her eyes after she realized I wasn't like Jacob. She's still a fighter somewhere deep inside, and that adds to her sexiness. But it's that same sexiness that makes me feel like hell. I shouldn't be thinking about her this way. I know what he did to her. I'm sure her sex appeal is the last thing on her mind, even if my body is telling me it knows what it wants.

I turn around, tossing back the rest of my scotch. "Yeah, I figured we could use a reminder of where we came from. Also, there might be a little bit of comfort in a cheeseburger for Sarah." I remember that back when she worked on set, she'd have a cheeseburger almost every day for her on-set lunch. I'm sure her dietician had a coronary over it, but she loved eating those fucking things.

"Sarah?" Marcus asks, surprised. "Didn't think you'd be calling her by name, at least not so quickly. What's going on, Ryker?"

"Just a moment," I reply, taking the bags of food from Marcus and putting a Big Mac, fries, Coke, and an apple pie in one of the bags, leaving the rest behind on the counter. "Let me take this to her. Fries fucking suck when they're cold."

Sarah's underneath the blanket when I come in, her dark eyes widening for a moment in panic before she remembers who I am. Maybe she was napping. I wouldn't be surprised after today's stress. "I have some dinner for you."

"And the clothes?" Sarah asks, and I see the balled-up ruin of her dress on the handcuff chain. "You said you'd bring me something."

"You're right. In all the stuff going on, that's slipped my mind. Eat, and then after dinner, I'll bring you something," I reply evenly, while on the inside, I'm kicking myself for forgetting. Most of the stuff I have won't fit her, but I've got an old pair of sweatpants that has a drawstring, and I can figure out something with one of my old undershirts. It'll be better than nothing. I hand her the bag and step back, letting her look inside. "Since we didn't know if you'd like our normal diet of filet mignon and caviar, we decided to go with burgers and fries. How's that sound?"

"Better than the filet," Sarah says honestly. "Jacob likes to eat that high-class shit. I'd rather eat a couple of sliders and—oh, my God."

"What?" I ask, and Sarah looks up with what looks like maybe gratitude in her eyes.

"Apple pie?" she says. "Haven't had one in so long. Jacob tends to control what I eat. He says . . . the last time I had a dessert outside of a restaurant, he didn't let me eat for two days."

I shake my head, more and more convinced that I'm doing the world a favor by killing this bastard. No one in the world should be deprived of apple pie. It's simple —Jacob Waters isn't human. Not that I needed any more motivation. "Then enjoy, because I'm nothing at all like him."

I close the door and go back out to the kitchen, where Marcus has already spread out our meals on the bar top, pulling up a couple of stools while he munches on a fry himself. "So . . .?"

"First, tell me how the boys are doing and the fallout so far," I order, setting his questions aside until after I have some food in my stomach. I really should have eaten earlier. A double scotch on an empty stomach is a bad idea, and my head feels a little swimmy after seeing Sarah's reaction to the apple pie. A fucking apple pie, and she was just this side of crying like a poor kid at Christmas getting their heart's deepest desire. What sort of monster is Jacob Waters anyway?

"We sent a runner to Waters's house. I sent along the anklet as proof we actually have her," Marcus says, making me nod. In all the chaos, that idea had slipped my mind. My brother makes me proud. He ad-libbed it perfectly. "The message was dropped off with the maid, which gave our boy a chance to get away. As for the crew that hit the funeral, we got our wounded man out of there, but the other two had to be left behind."

"They were good men," I reply, biting into my burger, but I'm unable to relish the taste. I can't help but feel responsible. I'm their leader. Sure, every man in today's crew was willing to die to get their licks in on Jacob Waters, but that doesn't mean I wanted to waste their lives like pawns in a chess game. I should have had a better plan. We shouldn't have lost anyone. "What about the streets?"

"Got them on lock," Marcus says. "The word is out— nobody moves and not a damn thing gets done. The crackheads are going to be feenin' for a hit by tomorrow."

"That's their fucking problem," I reply, trying a fry. It helps, the grease and salt and crispy texture helping lift my mood a little. "And the johns are just going to have to jack off for a night."

Marcus nods, sipping his Coke. "I got Big George downstairs in the lobby, perimeter security, but he can't stay there all night. And Kendra is ready to come in if we need her."

I smile at the mention of Kendra. She might be small, but that's one badass bitch. Miss five feet of fury herself, I've seen her take on guys a foot taller than her and knock them out. I'm more than happy with her covering my ass. "Call her in. Tell her and George to split the night. They can crash in the one spare bedroom we've got left up here when they're not on shift. Tomorrow, we can set up a regular security screen."

Marcus nods, chewing his fries. "So . . . Sarah?"

That's Marcus. He never forgets anything about me. I sigh, finishing off my burger before I look at my half-box of fries, setting them down for now. "You remember her? From years ago?"

"Remember her?" Marcus says, chuckling. "How the fuck wouldn't I? She was my teenage dream girl. Why?"

I shake my head, trying to calm myself. "You wouldn't believe what he did to her."

"What who did to her, Ryker?"

"Jacob. It . . . we've done a lot of shit that might not be good, but we're not evil, Marcus. That prick, though, deserves everything he's gonna get."

Marcus sits quietly, shocked as I tell him about the scars, setting his Coke down when I tell him about the deepest. "I mean, the fucking thing has shadows, Marcus! Shadows! Who the fuck does that to any woman, let alone their own fucking wife?"

"So, that's how she surprised you at the funeral," Marcus finally says, another gift of his where he often sets aside difficult conversation to come back to later. He doesn't forget. He just comes back later when the emotions aren't so strong. "She wasn't running from you because she knew who you were. She was running from him."

"Yeah. I bet she thought I was one of her husband's boys, trying to drag her back to him. Speaking of which . . ." I glance at the clock. It's getting late enough that I know exactly where Jacob Waters is going to be, the same place he is every night at this time. "Pass me the phone."

I don't have Jacob's personal cellphone, and I know his home line is going to be tapped by the boys in blue if he's called them in, but I doubt he has the brass to have the cops put a tracer on the phone line at The Waters Front, the restaurant and nightclub that makes up one of his supposedly legitimate businesses. There are four of them in the city, and they've been written up in *Food & Wine* magazine. He's very proud of them.

The phone rings three times, and when it's picked up, I can hear the strain in the voice on the other end. "The Waters Front. We're sorry, but due to unforeseen events—"

"Give me Jacob Waters," I interrupt the staffer. "Now."

"I'm sorry sir, but Mr. Waters—"

"Tell him that Ryker Johns is calling. And tell him that I have something of his that he wants very much."

The staffer stops, and when he speaks again, his voice sounds slightly strained. "Hold just a minute, please, sir."

I'm put on hold, subjected to the annoyance of Kenny G, and I pull the phone away from my ear a little. "I'm on hold."

"You sure about this, Ryker?" Marcus asks. "I mean, wouldn't a burner phone be better?"

"This way, he'll know for—" I start, but stop when the phone is picked up. "Hello, Jacob."

"You're a dead man," Jacob growls, and I'm at least partially reassured. He probably still thinks that I'm the same hoodlum my father was, street smarts, big balls, and not a lot more. "Dead, you hear me?"

"I could have killed you today," I reply, and Marcus sits back, listening in. "I was ten feet from you, and there was no way those three linebackers you had as your goon squad could have stopped me from putting one in your head. But I didn't. I want something else."

Here's the big lie, the part that I hope is going to keep Jacob a step behind until it's too late. The bait's out there . . .

"How much do you want for her? A million? Five?" Jacob asks, and I know I have him hooked. I can hear it in his voice. He might be a sadistic fuck of a husband, but he wants Sarah back. Badly. If for no other reason than to keep up appearances and for his own ego. There's no way he'd be tossing around money amounts so quickly otherwise.

"I wasn't even sure I was going to get her away from you, but now that I've got her, let's see. I got it. You know her last movie, Jacob? The one she filmed about six years ago, here in town?"

"Of course, I do. It's how I met her," Jacob grunts. "Why?"

"*Tears of The Young* grossed thirty-two million dollars. Not too bad, for a first-time leading actress. Tell you what, you give me exactly thirty-two million dollars, and you can have your wife back. I won't even worry about inflation or any small change that Wikipedia doesn't report."

"Thirty-two . . . are you fucking insane, Ryker? Or did you just get drunk off your ass before you called me?" Jacob asks, and I wonder for a second if I pushed my hand too far.

"Well, I can always keep her around for a while. She's not as fresh as she was ten years ago, mind you, but hey, she's still Sarah D. I can find a schoolgirl skirt like she used to wear," I tell him, even though the words make my hamburger turn in my stomach. Yeah, I want her, but it hurts to talk about her like that. I can't let Waters know though. "My brother and I wouldn't mind keeping her and sharing her. We'll remind her what it's like to be with a couple of studs."

"Wait!" Jacob screams, so loudly that even Marcus hears it. Someone who didn't know any better might think he actually cares about Sarah. "Listen . . . I just don't have that sitting around. I mean, even you gotta recognize that thirty-two million is a lot of fucking money. You don't just keep that sitting on your nightstand."

"We'll give you a few days to pull things together. Now, I know you probably don't exactly have all your shit saved down at the local Wells Fargo, so let's say a week. I'll call you then, and if you don't get it to me . . . she's mine."

I hang up before Waters can reply, then look at Marcus. "What do you think?"

"I think you should get the goddamn Academy Award," Marcus says with a look of admiration. "I've known you my whole life. I know how nobly you treat women. You sounded pretty fucking serious."

I chuckle, shaking my head. "Thanks, but you're right. Make sure everyone knows she is not to be abused. Nobody talks shit either. I was wrong about her. If I hear one motherfucker even make a dirty knock-knock joke with her, I'll send them off the balcony headfirst."

Marcus nods, not laughing at all. "Gotcha. Don't worry, that'll be passed on. So . . .?"

I sit back, looking at my now cold fries and pushing them away, picking up my Coke to finish it off. "So, Jacob Waters might be an abusive, shitty excuse for a husband, but he's obviously willing to play ball. That, or he's just buying time. I'd bet on the latter. So tomorrow, we start making our next moves. In the meantime, I've got something else to do."

"What's that?" Marcus asks, and I get up, going toward my bedroom. "Where are you going?"

"First, I'm going to take a piss," I reply, pausing at my bedroom suite's door. "Next, I'm going to get our guest some clothes like I promised her, and maybe a book."

Marcus laughs, shaking his head. "She always struck me as the paperback type. Got any Jackie Collins?"

I laugh, turning back toward Marcus, who's smiling broadly. He's always had the ability to help me laugh, even in the dark times. "Not quite my style. She might have to settle for Cormac McCarthy."

I'm picking through my old t-shirts when Marcus comes to my bedroom door, holding my phone. "Hey, Ryker?"

"Yeah?"

"The Narrows is on the phone. There's an issue that you need to take care of."

I look up, cursing under my breath. "What?"

"Small crew from Jacob Waters's group wanting to cross over to our side," Marcus says. "But they want to talk to the man."

I stifle my curse. I know this is what I wanted, even if the timing absolutely sucks. "Okay. Listen, grab my old sweats, the gray pair I used to wear, and one of my old t-shirts. Make sure Sarah's taken care of while I'm gone. Remember what I said."

Marcus nods while I reach for the drawstring on my casual pants, looking around for my jeans. They'll work with a sport coat and t-shirt for this. Hopefully, it won't take too long.

---

*T*he house looks like it should have been torn down years ago, and in probably any other city, it would have been. In this town, though, neighborhoods like the Narrows get nothing but delays and more crackhouses.

This house used to be one of those crackhouses too until it was chosen by the Narrows Niners as their headquarters. It still looks like it should be burned down, but that's beside the point tonight.

"You sure you want to go in there unarmed?" my escort, Skee-High, asks me. "I mean, the Niners are—"

"Are looking for reassurance they won't get cut down if shit kicks off," I reply. "They know the geography. They're surrounded by crews and sets that are part of our organization. That applies now too. They fuck up one hair on my head, and they know they won't see sunrise. Chill."

Skee still looks uncertain but follows as I approach the front door of the corner house. A light on the porch turns on, and before I can walk up the rickety steps, the door opens and the leader of the Niners, Nick Colvin, steps out. "Took you long enough, Ryker."

"Wanted to make sure your boys behaved themselves," I reply. "They've had eyes on us for blocks now."

"They do," Nick says. "The Niners can hold their own."

"True, but we both want the same thing, no more bloodshed for our people," I tell him. "So what do you say?"

I can see the pride in Nick's face. He's held out against me for a long time. And he's loyal too. He stayed with Waters because his gang's always been with Waters. Still, he's no idiot. Finally, Nick nods and steps away from the door. "Come on in . . . my friend."

CHAPTER 8

I shake at my handcuff, trying to figure out what to do. It's been a few hours since Ryker left, and while my left shoulder doesn't ache too much, I don't think I'm going to enjoy trying to go to sleep with my arm this way.

More than that, though, I just don't like being alone. I thought, after the way that I craved solitude in Jacob's house, that I was used to it. That I enjoyed being alone. Now, what I realize is that what I craved was safety, and the only way I was safe in that house was when I was alone. But now, with someone who may or may not be dangerous, I'm wanting company again.

There's a knock on the door, and before I can say anything, it opens. At first in the backlight, I think it's Ryker coming back, but then I see that the hair is a little bit shorter and styled differently. They're similar, but not quite the same. This man doesn't have quite as much force of personality in his movements as Ryker. Still, when he smiles, he looks friendly enough. "Hello."

"Hi," I say uncertainly. Hello? Not what I expect a street gangster to say . . . but what do gangsters say the first time they meet people? "Who are you?"

"The name's Marcus," the man says, bringing in a bucket. He sets it down before pulling out a pair of light sweatpants and a white undershirt. "Ryker was called away. He asked me to help you out with some things. So . . . let me help you with your sweats."

"I can do it," I reply defensively, not wanting him to touch me. Instead of arguing, he shrugs, handing me the sweats. It takes a little bit of fussing—I'm still handcuffed. Also, I've never put a pair of pants on one-handed before, but I don't give up, and Marcus is polite enough to turn his back the whole time. "Okay, now the shirt."

"You might be able to get it started, but I did a little life-hacking on the thing, so you might need help later," Marcus says, handing me the shirt. I see what he means. The entire left side and sleeve have been slit down the seam to let me pull it on one-handed without undoing the handcuff. Pretty ingenious, I gotta say, and I wonder about Marcus. Maybe he's the nice brother? Although Ryker wasn't that bad either. And Ryker is a lot more . . . magnetic than Marcus. There's something about Ryker that pulls at me, even as his brother's the one helping me out right now.

"Thank you," I finally say. "I can manage though."

Marcus smiles for a moment before it fades. "Okay, well, here's a bucket if you need it, and if you want a drink before I go to sleep, holler. I'll sleep out on the sofa. I'm a pretty light sleeper."

"Wait," I call as he goes to open the door. "Please, do you mind just staying to talk?"

Marcus turns and looks me over, and I get the same sense that I had when Ryker locked me up that there's something they're not telling me, like for some reason, I should know more about them than I do. Finally, though, he goes over and sits down on the small foot-locker against the wall, looking me over. "What do you want to talk about?"

"Well, your brother told me a little about why you guys took me, but I don't understand why. I mean, why are you guys doing this, trying to take down Jacob?"

Marcus leans forward, his face a little shocked. "You really don't know, do you?"

"Know what? Last time I said something about it, your brother damn near ripped my dress off. I'm kinda hoping to get some answers without repeating that."

Marcus sighs, sitting back and crossing his arms over his chest. It's only then that I see the gun at his waist, and I'm reminded that he's a criminal as well. "You first came to this city about six years ago to film a movie, right?"

"Yes," I answer. "My last movie. I think maybe I met your brother on set one day. He looks a lot like a security guy I met one day. I met Jacob Waters while I was working on the set too. We . . . uh, we dated while the film was in post-production and got married soon after."

Marcus nods. "Yeah, I've always wondered about that. Why'd you marry him anyway?"

I think back, trying to remember. It's almost like it was in another lifetime. "I guess I did it because I thought he was charming. I thought he was like what he showed to the public, a charismatic and tough dealing businessman. My agent introduced us, and I'll admit I was still young. I mean, being a teen actor makes you both jaded and overly innocent all at the same time. I was so used to hanging around and having so-called adult conversations with older people that when he showed romantic interest in me, I didn't even think about the fact that he was twice my age. And he is charismatic. He's cultured and apparently debonair, all the stuff you need to sweep an impressionable girl off her feet. He didn't start to show the other side of him until after we were engaged, and the abuse didn't start until after we were married."

I feel my face get hot, not in arousal but in shame as I look to the side. "It didn't take long for me to find out that I'd fucked up and married a monster."

Marcus shifts in his seat, and he looks angry. "So, what do you know about the rest of his work?"

74

"He's a crook, plain and simple. I guess that doesn't mean much to you guys, not with that gun on your hip, but it shocked me at first. Then as the time went on, I learned the hard way just how much control he has in this city. When the cops brought me home after the first time I ran away and he put the big scar on my back, I learned very fucking quickly," I say softly. "So yeah, if you two kill him, I'll be the first to celebrate."

"But you don't know about us, do you?" Marcus asks. He shakes his head. "You're sort of the reason that we're going after Jacob Waters. Our father was invited to one of the social events after you two got married. It was the one that, well, let's just say it was the garden party for those people who didn't want to get noticed by the newspaper."

"I remember that party," I reply, shivering. "It was that night that Jacob graduated from being just a little rough to actually hurting me. The next night was when I first told him no."

"Probably for the same thing that we hate him for," Marcus says sadly. "At that party, you met a man, about our height. He was just over forty at the time, kinda looks like us?"

I think back, nodding. "Yeah, I think so. But it all seems like it was so long ago. I think I remember him. He was the one person who made me feel like I wasn't just a side of meat to be paraded around. He actually listened to what I said, and when he smiled, it was a genuine one. It was after that smile that he said I reminded him of his sister."

"Our aunt," Marcus says, getting up. "Jacob thought that Pop was flirting with you, that he'd been disrespected. So, he had Pop dragged out of his own home by a couple of his thugs and then shot right in the parking lot of our apartment at the time. Ryker was staying the night. He was going to community college at the time to try and get into City. Our family, none of us had been to college, and Pop was so proud of him that he had us both over to throw Ryker a party. He insisted that his sons were going to be better than the street runner that he was, and Ryker . . . well, I was supposed to follow in Ryker's footsteps, but Ryker was first. Instead of pizza and beer, though, Ryker and I watched as Jacob blew our father's brains out all over the blacktop, then he just turned and got back in his BMW and drove away. The cops, of course, were in his pocket. They said that Pop was a suicide. How you commit suicide via gunshot wound to the back of the head, they never did explain."

I gasp, shocked at the story. "Your dad dying . . . he did that?" I swallow thickly, my throat going dry as a lump forms. "Jacob killed him because of me? And you thought I knew." I barely get the words out of my mouth. I feel like I'm breaking down, overwhelmed by sadness. "You must have thought I'm as much a monster as he is."

"We thought so," Marcus agrees, getting up. "Or at least

that you weren't innocent. But I can see in your face that you really didn't know. None of this is your fault at all. I'm not saying it's going to change your situation, but that's just the way things go."

"I guess," I reply, sighing. "Jesus, Marcus, I really didn't know. I'm just . . . I'm sorry about your father."

"Seems there's nothing you have to apologize for," Marcus says. "But thank you for it."

"So, what now?" I ask. "You know, now that I'm sort of stuck here for a while."

"Now?" Marcus asks. "Now, I'm going to set up your whiz bucket, Ryker's orders. If you need to do more, I walk you to the bathroom and back. Oh, and this."

Marcus reaches into the bucket again and takes out a book, handing it to me. "Sorry if it ain't your taste, but Ryker's the reader. I was always the guy who was more interested in video games and the streets than the books. Don't think that Ryker doesn't handle his shit either, though."

I look at the book, seeing that it's a Dean Koontz thriller. "Thanks, I guess. Sure you won't stick around a little longer?"

"Sorry, but I've got work to do, mainly making sure that you stay right where you are and keeping you safe," Marcus says. "Ryker's orders."

Marcus leaves, and I consider what he's said. I look at my bucket, and I wish I'd told him that I did need to use the toilet. It would have at least gotten me out of this bed for a while.

<hr>

A whole day later, and I've polished off the book and I'm bored out of my mind. Other than two more meals—oatmeal for breakfast, a ham sandwich for lunch—and two trips to the toilet, I've been stuck on this bed and the roughly two-foot quarter-circle that the chain and my left arm give me to move around the whole time.

This is worse than prison, maybe even worse than Jacob's. At least if I were in prison, I'd be allowed out to move around for part of the day. My eyes have done more moving than any other part of me in the past thirty-six hours. Even the digital clock on the other side of the room is maddening as it counts off the minutes of my capture.

The door rattles, and this time it's Ryker who comes in, carrying a bowl. "I've got dinner. Sorry I've been gone. I've been . . . well, working."

"Please," I beg, not wanting to but feeling broken down, "please let me go. I won't go back to Jacob. I won't tell him where you are or what you've told me, Ryker. Please."

"I'm sorry. I really am, but that's not going to happen," Ryker says, not brutally but with finality, setting the bowl down on the small table. "You're what's keeping me safe right now. Your husband has already begun taking steps to try to get you back. I thought I was being funny when I quoted thirty-two million for you, but apparently, he's trying to get it together."

"No!" I gasp, backing up. "No, please! Please!"

Ryker comes over, sitting down by my feet like he's ready to listen. In his deep blue eyes, I start to feel both empowered and ashamed. I'm embarrassed to look like this in front of this man. I want to be like the Sarah D. that he might remember. I want to . . . I want to feel worthwhile again, and in his eyes, I can see that he understands me, even before the words come out of my mouth.

"Ryker. I–I need a shower. I'm fucking filthy. And I need to get out of this room."

I don't mean to cry, I really don't. But within seconds, I'm bawling, sobbing as the idea of going back to that house fills my mind. Oh, God, poor Stanzie. What's Jacob been doing to her since I was taken? He's probably lashing out at everyone. I reach down, grabbing my half-ripped shirt, and wipe at my eyes before blowing my nose on the tail of the shirt. Looking at the disgusting mess that comes off, the makeup and lipstick and snot all mixing into a filthy mess, I don't even think as I peel it off, angry at this whole fucked up situation. "See? See what I've become?"

"I see that you're naked from the waist up," Ryker says in shocked amusement. He reaches out, and I think he's going to try and cop a feel before his finger rests on one of my scars. "Oh, Sarah."

"You see? I'd rather be your prisoner than go back there," I sob, the tears coming again. I find a dry, semi-clean spot on the rag in my hands and wipe at my eyes again. "But Ryker. I need to get a shower. I need to get all this filth off me. I need—"

Ryker takes his hand from my skin, his hand hesitant before he stands up. "I'm sorry, but you'll have to be patient with me about the shower."

"Why?" I half beg, half yell. "I won't try and run! I mean, strip me naked beforehand. I won't get anywhere that way!"

"It's not that," Ryker says. "The bathroom is a little out of order at the moment."

"What?" I ask. "You have a what, four thousand square foot penthouse? Don't you have more than one bathroom?"

Ryker nods. "I let my crew who's helping with security use the bathrooms. And some of these guys . . . they're my boys, but they're fucking stupid, to put it lightly. I guess there's a shared drain or something because everything's clogged. Marcus is out now to get a drain snake and some drain cleaner."

I can't help it, I start laughing. I don't know why. It's

not even funny. I guess it's just all the emotions going through me. Finally, I'm so breathless that I try to hug my knees, and my left arm rattles the chain on my handcuff, making me stop, sniffing at my armpit. "Let me know when I can."

Ryker nods then turns around. "Gimme a minute."

He leaves without another word, coming back a minute or two later with the handcuff key. "I wanted to make sure you've got privacy and a fresh t-shirt at least. Can't do much about the rest."

He unlocks the handcuff, and I can see he's tempted to cuff my other arm behind my back, but then he instead handcuffs himself to me. "One way to make sure you won't get up to any mischief."

"Mischief?" I ask. "And why would I get up to any mischief?"

"Oh . . . I seem to remember that your character loved to get up to all sorts of mischief," Ryker says. "I'm just making sure that fiction stays fiction."

Being so close to him, naked from the waist up, I can almost feel the magnetism of his presence pulling me toward him as we leave the bedroom. I can't help but check him out a little as we walk, and he's in phenomenal shape. Wide shoulders start the dramatic V-taper of his body, each muscle standing out against his skin, his arms rippling with muscle even through the long-sleeved shirt he's wearing. I can sense that he's got something on underneath, probably an undershirt of some kind, but it doesn't matter. I can see that he's built. He's right—he's nothing like Jacob. Inside me, a small voice wonders . . . but I don't really know this man.

We walk to the bathroom, where I can see a small pool of water in the shower stall. "I see what you mean."

"Yeah, well . . . be quick about it," Ryker says gruffly, and I think he's half embarrassed himself now. He grabs a washcloth and some body wash from the shower stall. "A sponge bath should be okay for now, right?"

I'm doubtful at first, but as I start to wash my face, it's wonderfully refreshing, and washing my body feels good too. As I wash, I can still feel Ryker's presence next to me, and I notice that he's looking at me with something that I haven't seen in a long time, so long that I'm not sure if I'm seeing things correctly.

I think it's genuine attraction, not the perverted power play that Jacob likes to playact instead of the real thing, and heat starts to creep up my cheeks as I wipe down my breasts, my nipples getting hard from the sensation.

"You know, it'd be a lot easier if you unlocked me," I rasp, trying to sound bitchy but failing when I see how he's looking at me. "I promise I won't run."

"I left the handcuff key in the bedroom," Ryker says half apologetically, but I can hear in his voice that he's not sorry. "I could help."

I consider it, then nod, handing him the wet washcloth. "Can you get my back and shoulders? And then maybe . . . turn around so I can finish?"

Ryker nods, lifting his arm so that he can stand behind me, our arms wrapped around my upper body. His hand rests on my stomach as he starts to wash, and while at first I feel self-conscious about his touching me, the warmth of his strong hand soon replaces it and I relax.

His touch on my back is gentle, almost a caress, and when my hips unconsciously push back, my ass bumps against something hot and hard.

Ryker stops, and I realize what I'm pressing against, both of us freezing stock still. Ryker's hand drifts up my stomach, cupping my breast, and the warmth of his fingers on my nipple sends tendrils of desire shooting through me, and I push back again, moaning this time. I stand up, turning around as best as the chain allows us, and look up at him. His face isn't filled with bitter hatred or the evil madness of Jacob, but instead with something purer, just normal desire.

Ryker pulls me closer and kisses me. His kiss has something that I thought was lost in the world, strength and tenderness in perfect balance, demanding but comforting. His tongue traces my lips, and I suck him into my mouth, moaning as his warm lips caress me and his free hand cups my ass through the sweatpants while my breasts crush against him.

I don't know what's driving me, but I can feel the rising desire to fuck him grow inside me. Maybe it's the way he looks at me or maybe it's the kind words or the fact that he hates my bastard of a husband. Or maybe it's just that Ryker's the sort of man I've always wanted, strong and virile, intelligent and powerful, but still, when he looks at me, there's respect in his eyes.

My hand is going down to find his cock when the door to the penthouse opens and I hear bootsteps in the hall. "Yo, Ryker! I got it!"

Marcus. Ryker lets go of me and steps back, both of us breathing a little heavier and Ryker looking a little guilty as he does so. He turns and goes to the door, sticking his head out. "Gimme two minutes!"

"Cool, bro," Marcus says, and I think he sounds amused, as if he knows something was going on between us.

I try to gather myself, my nipples still aching from the feeling of being pressed against his shirt, and my body is warm from his touch, but reality is setting in again. He is the man who kidnapped me, after all. And while his eyes might show respect, he's still just another criminal, the type of man I need to get away from. I should have learned a lesson, but maybe I'm drawn to the man who says he's going to kill my abuser, something I've longed to do myself for so long.

"Here, tuck this in your pocket," he says, reaching past me and opening the medicine cabinet, grabbing an unopened toothbrush. "I'll take you to my room and you can get a real t-shirt before dinner. You just have to promise not to try and shank me with it later."

After a quick trip through a walk-in closet that's outfitted with a surprisingly fashionable wardrobe that looks like he's ready for anything from Wall Street to 8-Mile in order to grab me a thicker if still plain t-shirt, we go back to my bedroom. Ryker unlocks the cuff from his wrist and lets me put my t-shirt on. When he doesn't move to lock me up again, I raise an eyebrow. "Are you setting me free?"

He shakes his head, getting the bowl from the dresser and handing it to me. "Sit. It's just canned beef stew with rice, but it's better than a Value Meal. I'll stay, and then after you're done eating, I'll lock you back up."

The chance to use my left arm again is unexpectedly pleasant, and as I dig into the beef stew, I smile. "I guess you and your brother aren't gourmets."

"I love good food," Ryker counters, sitting at the end of the bed and watching me with his intense blue eyes. "I just can't cook very well. Still, I do enjoy going out when I have the free time. Maybe in the future, I'll learn how to make something good. You know, when I retire or something."

His light attempt at gallows humor makes me smile a little, and I keep eating, relishing every bite. Too quickly, the bowl is empty and I've scraped out almost every droplet of liquid inside. I hand it back to him, aware more than ever of his eyes on me. "Thank you. Might not be on Yelp, but it was good."

"You're welcome." Ryker stands up, and I'm less resistant this time to watching the cuff close on the bedpost. "Is there anything else you'd like?"

"A new book?" I ask. "I finished what Marcus gave me. Something a little different this time, if you have it."

Ryker picks up the Koontz book, chuckling. "Okay, I'll see what we have."

He reaches for the door, and I speak up again. "Ryker?"

"Yeah?" Ryker asks, turning back.

I shake my head, looking down. "I just wanted to say I'm sorry. Last night, Marcus told me about your father. I'm sorry that he got killed."

Ryker's hand falls off the doorknob and he turns the rest of the way around. "Thank you," he whispers. "He wasn't a perfect man or even a perfect father, don't get me wrong. But he loved us, and Jacob Waters shot him in the back of the head while he knelt in the street. I'll never forgive him for that."

I'm struck by the intensity of the emotion in his voice, and I swallow, looking down. "I'm sorry I got him killed. I was thinking over the past day, and I do remember him. It just took me a while. He was . . . he was just being nice to me. And when he said I looked like your aunt, he said it so bashfully, I sort of kissed him on the cheek. He was just being cute and I was so happy. I gave him a peck, and he turned so red it made me laugh. I didn't know that Jacob—"

Ryker comes over and lifts my chin, looking me in the eyes. His voice is driving, piercing me to my very soul and reassuring me. In his voice I hear not just power, but respect, and his eyes speak to the very depths of my soul. "You have nothing to apologize for. My hatred is reserved for one man only. When his city is my city and his blood is on my hands, that hatred will be satiated. But thank you for telling me. I'll bring you a book later."

CHAPTER 9

RYKER

*a*fter dropping off another book to Sarah, this time *American Gods,* I go out to the living room, where I find Marcus blowing his nose and wiping at his eyes. "You okay?"

"Yeah . . . just that drain cleaner smells fucking terrible!" Marcus says, chuckling. "I poured a bottle in each shower, and then the fumes hit me. Felt like something had reached up and grabbed my brain and was pulling it out through my fucking nostrils!"

I go over to the kitchen garbage, where I see the bottles in the trash, and I pick one up, checking the instructions. "Holy shit, man, you're lucky to be alive. This is the industrial-grade shit and on the back, it says you're supposed to wear a ventilator and goggles when you pour it. Where the hell did you get it?"

"Louie's Plumbing Supply," Marcus says. "You know, the company owned by Downtown Bootsy's brother?"

I nod, putting the bottle carefully back in the trash before washing my hands in the sink. Better safe than sorry. I'd like to not dissolve my eyeball next time I get an itch. "Be careful with that shit. And the rest of what you went out for?"

"Streets are still on lock, man. The dealers are ready to pay directly to us, and the street workers are too. The Docks are ours already, and it might take a while, but I think we can get the airport under us quickly too. With some pressure."

I nod, thinking as I pour myself a cup of coffee. "Okay, we'll focus there. Anything from Jacob?"

"Just what you heard. He's supposedly raising the money somehow. He's called in markers with a lot of people. Word is he wants her back bad."

I shake my head. "Maybe, but I was wrong about her."

"About Sarah?" Marcus asks as I pour him a cup of coffee and hand it to him. "How so?"

I sit down, trying to separate my logical thoughts from the physical memories of having her pressed against my body, her lips on mine as we kissed in the bathroom. She was perfect, the way her skin felt, the weight of her breast in my hand, the feel of her lips on mine. I've had women before. It sort of comes with my position in life. But none of them kissed me the way that

Sarah did, and none of them felt the way she did in my arms. Even now, I'm having trouble trying to control the urge to go back to her room and give her what her body demanded, and what my body needs as well. I want to fuck her, to feel her underneath me and to hear her gasp, whining as I set her body on fire. I want to show her what sex really can be, and what it could be. What I want to give her, and what I want to take from her.

"When we talked about snatching her, it was not just to paralyze Jacob. We assumed she was guilty too," I finally say, sipping my coffee. "But we were wrong. We thought she was involved, that she had to know. You said it yourself."

"I also said I thought she was too stupid to realize what she'd become involved in," Marcus recalls. "I talked to her last night, and she isn't stupid."

"And a lot more innocent than we are," I finish.

"She is. Somehow, I never expected that, but she's the one person in all of this who might really be innocent. So what are we doing, Ryker? We could take the money and still not return her to that abusive asshole," Marcus says, looking thoughtful.

"It ain't about the money. It never was. It's about respect and fear," I reply. "He could go to the governor himself and tell him to hand over the entire state budget, and so long as Jacob's got respect and fear on his side, the governor's going to ask if he wants a blowjob along with the cash. No. He might lose a little respect, but I doubt it. If anything, he's upping the fear levels people have of him. He's gotta show that he won't let anybody take from him what belongs to him, or else he loses something more important than the damn money. The stakes are getting higher and higher between us each minute, and it's going to come to blood sooner rather than later."

"So, what do you want to do?" Marcus asks, and I think, sipping my coffee. It's hard to think suddenly. All of my thoughts about Jacob are mixed up with my thoughts about Sarah and the way she felt in my arms. It felt so right, but I have to wonder if it was only because she is *his*. Finally, I come to a conclusion.

"First, no more negotiations. I don't care if he offers thirty-two, sixty-four, or a hundred and twenty-eight million dollars for her. This is all over, and he ain't getting her back. Fuck him and his money. No, we go after him and take away his respect and fear," I say harshly, finishing off my coffee. "And I want his four restaurants hit. Not just hit. I want them blown the fuck up. Waters is proud of those fucking restaurants, they're like his crown jewels when he wants to pretend he's a legitimate businessman. So we take those away from him. For now, though, I'm going to go get a fucking workout in, get rid of some stress."

I stand, going to my room, where I quickly change. I've got my own gym in the basement of the building, so that's not a problem for security as I leave my bedroom and head toward the elevator. I pause at the door, looking back at Marcus, who's pulled up a kung fu movie on the computer. "Hey, Marcus?"

"Yeah?" Marcus says, taking out his earbuds. "You want the computer for something first?"

"No, not that. Just . . . what I don't understand is why he treated her like that if he's willing to pay up. Why would he treat such a beauty that way?"

Marcus shakes his head, putting his right earbud back in but leaving the video paused. "Beats me. You're the one who took philosophy and read that Roman fucker and shit. For me, I guess it comes pretty simple."

"What's that?" I ask as Marcus turns back to the computer but still pauses to answer.

"Some men are just monsters. Have a good lift."

Some men are just monsters. He might not be Marcus Aurelius, but my brother says some pretty wise things sometimes.

CHAPTER 10

"*I*t's been days. Please, just let me go," I plead. I can't stand it anymore. It's not the way I've been treated, other than being stuck to the bed. Most of the time, Ryker and Marcus have treated me well, with respect even.

It's the stress. Every minute, I expect to hear gunfire or an explosion, or something signaling Jacob coming to get me. I can barely sleep. I haven't been able to move enough to really wear myself out, and with nothing but books and boredom to fill my hours, my inner demons have come out to play. I want to do anything to get away from them, especially the fear. It doesn't matter that Ryker is nice to me or that he's so handsome, or that when he looks at me, there's respect in the desire in his eyes. It doesn't matter that my body wants him too. I'm terrified of the ghost around the corner.

"You can't just keep me here forever. He's going to find

you, and then . . . please, he'll kill us both after this long. He's a fucking psycho."

"I know that," Ryker says. "But I'm not letting you go, Sarah. I did a quick little remodeling job, though. I have a secure room for you."

He comes over and unlocks the handcuff, not at the bedpost like he's always done before but at my wrist. Rubbing at my wrist, looking at the light pink mark there, I follow him to the elevator, where he takes me downstairs. It feels longer than when I was over his shoulder, and when the door opens, I see why. "We're underground."

"Exactly," Ryker says. "I own a lot more than just the penthouse of this building. And the other day, after our talk, I did a lift down here. While I was in the middle of it, I realized I had a better, more secure place than locking you up in a spare bedroom all day."

Ryker takes out a key and unlocks a door, and I'm surprised by what I see. "Uh . . . it's a cell."

He looks around, humming. "I suppose you can see it that way."

See it that way? The walls are cinderblock, the vaulted heights of the penthouse have been replaced by a ceiling just a few inches above my head, and the rich carpet's been replaced by what looks like industrial carpeting. While there's a cabinet, there isn't a lot more unless the corner section that's covered by a moveable curtain is hiding something special. "How could I see it any other way? Ryker, there are no windows."

He nods, leading me inside and closing the door behind us. "Of course there aren't. That wouldn't be very secure now, would it? But there's also no chains in this room. Back in the day, this used to be the office for the maintenance guy back when he lived on site. You've got running water and a toilet."

Ryker shows me the curtained off area, and he's right, and while the toilet's old-looking, it's in decent shape and the water flows clear at least. "Better yet, check this out."

He opens the cabinet, and I'm surprised to find a TV with a PlayStation attached. "It's an older one. There's no Internet on this thing, but one of my boys brought it over along with a dozen games. Between that and any books you might like, you'll find what you need to keep your mind occupied, and there's enough space that you can get some exercise in and let your body get the kinks out all you want. Best of all, like I said, no chains."

I look around, nodding. "It's better than being chained up, I guess. I'd rather have my freedom, but I'll take it."

Ryker shakes his head, a little frustrated. "Sarah, do you know what's going on out on the streets right now? It's an underground war that's starting. Nobody's taking prisoners right now. If I let you go, at worst, he may very well find you and kill you. At best, you go back to him. He knows where you are, and in this kind of war, it's not about hiding but about keeping your enemy afraid to hit you. Right now, he's afraid of not getting you back. If I let you go, make no mistake, he will find you. I'm not going to let you get yourself killed."

The way he says it makes me shiver, fear rippling down my spine. Ryker is right. Running away is a fool's errand, but still, why should I feel so grateful for being given a goddamn cell instead of being locked up?

"Well, can I at least take a shower now?" I ask, sniffing. A washcloth helps, but I still feel pretty ripe and grungy. That, more than anything else, is adding to my feeling of ungratefulness. One luxury Jacob did allow me was long, warm showers. It helped me deal with the stress. "You know, with soap? You should have gotten the drains cleared by now."

Ryker stops, then nods brusquely. "Fine. There's a shower down here you can use."

He opens the door, leading me down the hallway to another room, which I find is a decently equipped home gym. "Yours?"

"Mine," Ryker agrees, leading me to a door on the far wall. "Here."

It's a small locker room with a shower stall large enough for two or three people. Simple but effective. "I'll make sure that you're given another change of clothes and some toiletries," he says as he sits down in the folding chair. "Go ahead."

I look around, surprised. "There's no changing stall. There isn't even a shower curtain."

"Never needed one," Ryker says simply. "As for you, I've seen it all already."

I nod, for some reason nervous as I take off my clothes and get in the shower. The water's nice and warm, a luxury after being dirty for so long. I let the water run over my neck and over my face, trying to remember that Ryker's right. He's seen me naked from the waist up before. But as the warm water runs over my body, I can feel his eyes on me, and I look back, shaken by the intense look on his face.

"Don't worry about me. Just wash yourself," Ryker says, and I turn back, trying my best to do just that, to put the fact that he's right behind me out of my mind. But then he stands up, and I'm startled, dropping the soap. I bend down to pick it up, dropping it again when I hear something hit the floor. I turn around and see that he's in the shower with me.

He's gorgeous, even more than I thought he could be. His body isn't bulky but rather lean, his muscles long and flowing from joint to joint. If he weren't a gangster, he could be a male model with a body like his. His hips are slim, but there's still corded muscle below his washboard stomach, and when I look down, I gasp.

His cock is long and thick, and I can't stop my mind from thinking what he could do to me with it. For all the brutality that Jacob's put me through, he's never been able to measure up, and looking at Ryker, I gulp. My mind fills with heat, the thoughts of what an encounter with him could be. It would change me forever, regardless of what happens after this, but I want it. I want the change. I look up into his eyes, and he's looking at me with such intensity that I know he's thinking the same thing.

"I've watched you for days," Ryker says softly, taking me by the shoulders and turning me around. His fingers start to stroke my skin, and I feel laid bare, unable to resist the fact that he's touching me more intimately than when he teased my breasts the other day. "You're beautiful, Sarah."

"You don't know what you're talking about," I whisper.

"You're a survivor," Ryker says. "And the only scars you ever need to worry about are the ones on your soul."

I turn to him, more vulnerable than I've felt in years. "I'm scared, Ryker."

"I'll keep you safe," he says, and suddenly, we're kissing, his hands roaming over my body as the warm water pelts my back. I'm kissing him back, our tongues and lips dueling as I feel myself wake up more. Five years, and this is what I've been missing. Heat, pure and wonderful. Desire, not fear, and it feels like warm honey dribbling down my throat and sweetening every taste in my mouth. Ryker's lips trail down my neck as he bends his knees slightly, his hand coming to squeeze my ass, and he kisses over my shoulder before going back to my lips, drawing my breath into him and sharing everything with me.

He pushes me back against the side wall of the stall. The tile's a little cold, but that just makes it all seem real. This isn't some just fantasy I've imagined after Jacob's abusiveness. This is real. This man who's holding me and kissing me is completely real. "Ryker . . . oh, my God, you're really doing this."

"Aren't I the one who's supposed to wonder if I'm in a fantasy?" he asks with a confident chuckle as he steps back, bringing his hand up to cup my left breast, kneading it and making my knees weak. "You're the one who was my teenage fantasy. I even fantasized about you when I was your security guy."

"I wondered if that was you. With the creepy fan?" I ask, my head spinning as the steamy shower combines with the words he's murmuring in my ear and the feeling of his hand on my breast.

"That was me. I'll admit, I spent a few weeks after that with daydreams of you running around in my mind. The way you looked at me . . ." Ryker says before his tongue finds my earlobe and I'm swept away in the feeling of his hands on my breasts and his tongue on my skin. Each sweep is electric, his fingers lightly pinching my nipples until they're hard and aching even under the warm water, the warmth and wetness between my legs having nothing to do with the shower at all. "The way you looked at me made me fantasize about what could have been. Now, I have it. Sarah, I'm going to fill you up, slide my cock so deep inside you that you're going to feel split open. But you're going to want it, aren't you? You're going to beg for me to give it to you, to show you what being with a man is supposed to be again. I'm going to take you, make you come on me, and shake you to the very depths of your soul. I'm going to remove the damage that he's done to you, and when I'm done, you're never going to be the same again. That's what you want, isn't it?"

I can't even reply. His words take the breath right out of my mouth. Instead, I reach down blindly, tracing my fingernails over his hard stomach to find his cock, which is now fully hard and throbbing in my hand. Even just touching him feels like I'm being swept away, the veiny texture and the thick flare of his cockhead sending my body into tremors of anticipation. I've never, in my whole life, felt a cock like this before, and to be honest, it scares me a little. He's right, this is going to change me once this is over. Ryker notices, and his lips pause before he pulls back. "Sarah?"

"You realize how fucking hung you are?" I ask, stroking him lightly. "It's a little intimidating, Ryker."

He ignores me, pinning me against the wall and lifting my leg, his eyes boring into mine. "Are you saying no?"

"No way in my life am I saying no to—" I start, but then all the words are ripped from my mind as his cock fills me. I feel him go slowly at first, and my pussy accepts him without protest, white-hot pleasure rolling up my spine as he fills me in one long, slow stroke. I grip him, my fingers digging into his shoulders as he goes deeper, deeper than anyone's ever gone before, and it starts to hurt a little as I'm stretched, but I don't care. It's the good kind of hurt. I grab his head, kissing him when he buries himself all the way to the hilt inside my body.

We go slowly at first, Ryker's cock sliding in and out of me at a sensual pace, our lips and hands stroking our bodies as he gives me time to adjust, or maybe he's just taking in the luxury of being inside me. After a moment, he cups my cheek, looking me in the eyes. "So . . . fucking . . . perfect."

His tone is even better than the feeling of his cock rubbing against all the right places inside me, the head of his cock touching places I didn't even know existed inside me and my clit grinding against him slowly. "You . . . thank you. Faster?"

Ryker grunts lightly, pulling out and turning me around, pulling my arms behind my back, and throwing my hair out of the way so that his lips can find my neck while he buries himself inside me again. His cock drives into me at a harder, more demanding angle that lights up my pussy in a whole different way. I didn't know it could be this way as he pumps in and out of me, letting go of one arm to knead my breasts, his breath hot on my ear. "Is this what you want? Harder?"

"Oh, fuck, yes," I moan, my eyes closing as Ryker lets go of my breast to hold onto my arms, pulling me back into him and letting me bend over. His cock hammers me, my pussy squeezing him, and my body is inundated with explosions of pleasure. I'm lost, the two of us moving together as his cock and his . . . his everything pours into me, every slapping thrust of his hips against my ass tearing away the hurt inside me and opening me up raw.

I'm sobbing, half in joy and half in fear as Ryker slams into me again and again, both of us groaning and making nonsensical sounds as I'm overloaded, leaping into a level of pleasure that I've never felt before. It keeps building bigger and deeper until it feels like with every stroke of his cock, Ryker is connecting directly with my brain. My body is just a conduit for the overwhelming sensation that suddenly breaks, and I'm coming, my pussy clamping on his cock as I raise my face to the shower spray and scream, the water the only thing keeping me from passing out as he swells and shoots deep inside me, blast after blast of his come that somehow makes it feel all the better, like for the first time in my life, I'm an actual woman and not something else.

My knees give out but Ryker grabs me quickly, holding me in his arms as he cradles me, carrying me out of the shower and into the changing area, where he lowers us to the floor carefully, holding me like a child in his arms as I sob, overwhelmed by everything.

"Shh, it's okay," he whispers, stroking my arm and

holding me still. "I've got you, Sarah. You're safe here. I promise you, I'll keep you safe."

"Why?" I whisper between sobs. "You barely know me. You . . . I hurt you, I hurt your brother, but—"

"Because you are a good person, better than scum like me, and you never asked for any of this," Ryker says gently. "Because you deserve better than what you've had, and you deserve better than this."

"And when Jacob pays?" I ask. "What then?"

"I'm not sending you back to him," Ryker promises me. "After Jacob Waters is dead, I'm giving you your freedom. I swear it."

His promise brings fresh sobs to the surface for some reason, although I don't know why. Maybe it's that I'm grateful for someone promising me my freedom, but there's another part of me that doesn't want to be free. It wants to stay right here in these powerful arms, regardless of what else happens.

As the water dries and the warmth from the steam chills to just the warmth of his body, I realize something that's scaring me. I'm starting to feel for Ryker Johns. It's fucked up, I know it is, but there's something about him. If only I'd had a chance to actually talk with him again on the set. If only I hadn't met Jacob. How much different would my life have been?

CHAPTER 11

"We've got everything ready," Marcus tells me while we ride through the streets in a nondescript gray Toyota in order to blend in. I don't like leaving Sarah behind, but I've got three good men on security at the building, two in the lobby while one is right outside her door, and it can't be helped.

"Good," I reply, picking up my phone as we hang a right. "Then let's make the call. Are we near any of the restaurants?"

"The Waters of Meribah," Marcus says, pointing at the in-dash screen. "About a mile away."

"Cool, put us a half block beyond the thing so we can drive away easily," I tell him, dialing Jacob. I'm on a burner phone this time. I don't want this particular call tracked. But not for the reasons some people might suspect. If the cops are listening in by now, they'll help me out. A rep of their union approached my people, and they're ready to talk once Jacob's out of the way.

"Hello?" a woman's slightly accented voice asks. The Waters of Meribah is Jacob's neo-Persian restaurant, and from what I hear, it's quite good.

"Jacob Waters, please. Tell him it's Ryker Johns."

The hold is less this time than when I called his restaurant, and when he picks up, I can hear the anger and frustration in Waters's voice. "What do you want, you prick? You said a fucking week!"

"Decided to up the timeline," I reply, not worried when a little bit of anger creeps into my voice. There's a time to be ice cold, and there's a time to be angry. Besides, this bastard deserves anger and more. "Some of your boys in blue and other crews have been giving mine a hard time."

"You son of a bitch! I swear I'm going to—" Jacob starts, his voice rising again, and I cut him off brutally.

"What you're going to do is call your restaurants and tell them to clear the fuck out. If they're not out in exactly . . . six minutes from now, they're going to be dead in a big pile of dust," I finish for him. "Those deaths are going to be on your head, not mine. Hope you have them on speed dial."

I hang up, waiting for a second to see if he'll waste time

trying to call me back while at the same instant, Marcus speaks into his phone. "Dial now."

He hangs up, looking over at me. "Okay, they're getting the warning calls. Hope they take us more seriously than Waters has."

I watch as people start to stream out of the restaurant, mostly workers, but there are a few late patrons as well. I don't want innocents hurt, and that includes workers who most likely are just schlepping food in a restaurant to make ends meet. I may be making a mistake trusting that this psycho will tell them, but I hope not.

"Thirty seconds," Marcus says softly, and I'm grateful as the crowd slows to a trickle then stops, a few standing around across the street, wondering. Idiots, there's always someone who wants to just watch things blow the fuck up, but there's nothing I can do about that now. I lift the cover on the trigger. I might have told Jacob it was on a timer, but I wanted to do this myself just in case, to ensure no innocent casualties. "Three. Two."

I trigger the bomb a second early, a Claymore mine that one of my crew planted near the natural gas lines that feed the water heater and the cooking ranges. The explosion ignites the spewing gas, turning the whole back of the restaurant into a gigantic fireball that builds before the roof tears off, the doors following a second later to fly across the street. I squint at the glare and pat Marcus on the shoulder. He drives off without a word, turning left and bringing us back toward the freeway. We're on the onramp when my phone rings and I see that it's Jacob Waters.

"I don't fuck around, Jacob. You should know that by now. What do you want?"

"You son of a bitch," Jacob says with his usual greeting. It seems he doesn't have much of a vocabulary when he gets angry. His voice is low and deadly this time, though, more collected instead of just yelling. I raise an eyebrow. This is the Jacob Waters that I've been looking for. I've gotten past all his bullshit, all his shields, all his buffers. This is the man I want to hurt, the man who casually slaughtered my father and put Sarah through hell. "I'm going to make you beg me to kill you, motherfucker."

"Call me names if you want, Jacob, but you know the old playground chant? They'll never hurt me," I reply, keeping my voice level. I'm both excited and, to be honest, a little scared. I'm excited because not only am I hurting the real Jacob Waters, but I'm pitting myself against the man who has run this city and most of this state for over two decades. But that's scary too, and I momentarily wonder . . . have I fucked up in my thinking? Is my army of the streets enough to take him down? Is there a variable I'm not accounting for? "I think we have an understanding, don't we?"

"Oh, I understand just fine," Jacob says, his voice still a deadly whisper. "I understand that you won't be able to go home again. That little forty-eighth story penthouse of yours? That fucker's going to be destroyed by the end of the night. You know, I spent a whole day trying to think of why you'd be so fucking stupid as to try and take me on this way. Then I remembered. Your old man. I killed him like the bitch he was."

"You might just be right," I concede, not letting him piss me off. "Of course, the reason could be even simpler. Maybe I just think it's time for this city to have a new king."

Jacob laughs, something that worries me more than any scream of rage or threat he could make. Laughter means he's still somewhat in control of himself, and that is dangerous. When you're in control, you think. When you think . . . you're deadly. "If you think you're man enough, boy, I guess we'll find out. Fuck it, I guess I'll just have to move on to wife number four before I turn fifty-five."

The line goes dead, and I look at Marcus. "Get us home, now."

"Ryker . . ." Marcus starts, but he stops when he sees my face. "Take a moment and think, man. He wouldn't kill her. He wants her back. He needs her back to show he's still the man."

"If she goes back to him, she's as good as dead," I reply. "I get her out and you get the shit from the penthouse that we can't lose. Then we boogie for the safe house."

*T*he back of the van is packed, five guys along with me and Sarah. She didn't even have time to really change. She's wearing one of my old sweatshirts along with the sweatpants and a pair of shower sandals while she looks around worriedly. I sit next to her, and when she puts a tentative hand on my leg, I take it and give it a reassuring squeeze. "You'll be safe," I whisper. "It won't be as comfortable, but you'll be safer than if you were in Fort Knox."

Henry, one of the guys in the back, keeps looking over at us, mostly at Sarah, and it pisses me off the way he's looking her up and down. He's looking at her like she's a piece of meat, something he wants to fuck just so that he can have a story to brag about in the bar. He doesn't look at her like she's a real woman, a woman with hideous scars underneath the sweatshirt she's wearing, a real woman who's scared shitless and whose only comfort in the entire world right now is me, and to a lesser extent, my brother. Even worse, he's looking at her like maybe it'd be easier for us to just get rid of her, to get rid of the distraction so we can focus on taking down Waters.

He just doesn't understand how everything that I want to do, that keeping Sarah free, and letting her be free from the hell she's been through, is just a miniature version of the entire reason I'm on this fool's errand. Finally, after the third time, I get pissed off enough to say something. "There a fucking problem, Henry?"

"Uh . . . no, Boss. No problem at all," Henry says, looking down suddenly before looking up. "No disrespect. Just . . . Miss D, I wanted to say I liked your TV show."

Sarah looks over, smiling slightly. "How old are you?"

"Nineteen," Henry says, fidgeting. "Why?"

"Aren't you a little young to remember that?" Sarah asks. "There's no way they play it on the air now."

Henry blushes, looking down. "My big sister really liked the show, too. And it's on daytime cable now."

Sarah nods, then looks at me. "Oh, yeah. I forgot about syndication. Where old shows never die."

"Either way, let's keep our heads in the game," I say gently to Sarah before giving Henry a hard look. "Got it?"

Henry nods, and I hold my tongue. He's normally an okay kid.

"We're getting close," Marcus interrupts from his traditional shotgun seat spot, again with a shotgun between his legs. "The advance party should be there already."

It takes us another five minutes before the van makes the final turn and pulls into the safe house, a warehouse in the Docks that is in the middle of a block that my men control more than any other in the city. Even more than the neighborhood that I started with, the Docks is the closest thing we have to a fortress island.

For almost four years, my word has been law in the Docks, and everyone here has benefited for it. To a man, the Docks would die for me, and the whole city knows it.

"There's going to be people here," I tell Sarah softly. "But they're here for your protection. Okay?"

"Okay," Sarah says softly, giving my hand another squeeze before entwining her fingers in mine. "For luck."

The van comes to a stop, and Marcus hops out, already hollering orders. "All right, get the door closed and get this fucking place locked down tight! Locals, I want your asses out on the streets making sure not a single motherfucker who ain't part of our crew comes within a half mile of this spot. I don't care if it's fucking Santa Claus going for a jog with the Pope!"

"I didn't think he could be so commanding," Sarah says softly in amazement, and I have to chuckle.

"Marcus is only a teddy bear around the house. Don't worry, it's something he's good at. He does most of the yelling for me . . . usually."

The crew scatters, and Marcus turns around. "What else do you need, Ryker?"

"Let's get Sarah over to her bed, then we need to have a powwow," I reply, leading her over to the office area. It's not as comfortable as her 'cell', but she'll be safe here. Inside, there's an old metal-frame Army surplus bed with a decent mattress, sheets, and a wool blanket. "Here, catch some shuteye."

"Like that'll happen," Sarah says nervously. "I'm a nervous wreck and—"

I close the door and pull her close, kissing her hard and cutting off her words. She's stiff at first before she melts into my arms, and when her tongue touches my lips, I open up to her, tasting her delicious natural flavor for a moment before releasing her. "Better?"

"A little," she admits. "Where'd you learn how to do that so well?"

"Lots of fantasies of some hot chick on TV who liked to wear a schoolgirl outfit," I tease. "I'll be right next door in the meeting room, talking to Marcus. You've got an army protecting you tonight, and even if Superman himself got through them, he'd have to take out me and Marcus to get to you."

"I'd put money on you two," Sarah says before sitting down on the bed and stretching out. Sarah wiggles her bare feet as she does so, and I'm reminded that she only had some cheap shower sandals, a total no-go in this building. It used to be a legit warehouse, and after that a chop shop. There's metal shavings and more all around this place.

"Thanks. Oh, but I need to ask . . ." I say, turning around. "Shoes? What size?"

"Ten in women's," Sarah says. "Sorry, I've got big feet."

"You know what they say about women with big feet, right?" I quip, and Sarah grins, shaking her head. "They need big socks."

"They got it mostly right," Sarah says. "At least it rhymes the same."

I laugh and leave the room, closing the door behind me. Entering the 'office,' I turn to see Marcus already waiting for me at the table, a can of generic cola in his hand and one awaiting my attention at the head of the table. I can use the caffeine and sugar right now. My smile disappears, and I sit down. "Everyone in place?"

"They're pros, Ryker. As much as street gangsters can be. She's in good hands."

I crack the can, drinking deeply as I try to calm down, but I can't. "Where the fuck is he?"

"I don't know," Marcus says. "The war's about to go very fucking hot after what we did. We knew this was going to happen, though. That's why we prepped this place."

"Yeah . . . still," I rasp, crumpling the now empty can after draining it. "I'm worried about the beast we woke up tonight. No, fuck that, the beast *I* woke up tonight."

"You're stronger than he is," Marcus says. "If you think you're compromised—"

"Why would I be compromised?" I ask sharply, and Marcus raises his hands. I take a deep breath, calming myself. Marcus is more than my brother. He's the one person I can trust to tell me the truth all the time. "No, tell me what's on your mind."

"Nothing, Ryker. I'm just saying . . . if you're worried about time, maybe we need to take him out now," Marcus says. "Put the word out and make some motherfucker rich for his head."

I shake my head, slamming my fist on the table. "No! I want to do it. He made Pop kneel and die with no honor. His blood belongs to me. Where is he now?"

"We've got people looking for him," Marcus says. "Like us, though, he's got to have safe houses, probably ones a lot more comfortable than ours. Knowing our luck, the fucker's in some five-star hotel downtown, sipping on Dom."

"If he is, then I'll shove the whole bottle down his throat," I growl, but what goes through my mind isn't the image of my father dying but the sight of Sarah's panicked eyes when she begged me not to let her go back to him and the feel of her skin under my fingers as we were in the shower. Either way, the fucker deserves to die. "Put the word out—fifty grand to whoever gives us his confirmed location. But nobody moves on Jacob Waters without my say so."

Marcus nods, standing up. Before he can go, I reach out, taking his wrist. "That means you too, Marcus. I lost a father to this asshole. I won't lose my brother, too."

He looks like he's about to protest, but he knows it's

useless. We've had this discussion before, and I'm not changing my mind. I'm the elder brother, and while that might sound old-fashioned as hell, I'm the one with the right of vengeance. Still, it burns Marcus, and he opens his mouth to say something when his phone rings and he takes it out. "Huh, didn't think he'd call. Not after all this time."

"Who?" I ask, and Marcus shows me his phone. "Joe Strauss? What the hell is he calling for?"

Joe Strauss is one of the best hitmen in the city, and perhaps one of the top ten in the entire country. His biggest advantage is that he doesn't look like you'd expect a hitman to look. He's not tall, he doesn't look athletic, and in fact, he's nearsighted to the point that if he ever got into a hand-to-hand fight with someone, he'd probably get his ass handed to him. He looks more like an accountant or a dentist than a hitman. But that's one of his biggest advantages, too, because nobody sees him coming until it's too late. It's been two years since I last talked to him, and I wonder what brings him back into my life now.

"Hello, Joe?"

"It's nice to hear your voice, Ryker. Thankfully, your brother never changes his damn phone number, unlike you, Mr. I Love Burner Phones," he says in his pleasant, middle-class sounding voice. Listening to him, I can understand why he's a junior high school teacher in his normal life. "How are you doing?"

"If you've kept your ear to the ground, Joe, you'd know how I'm doing," I reply sarcastically. "What can I do for you?"

"It's not what you can do for me, but what I can do for you," Joe says. "I just got a call from a representative of Jacob Waters. The man wants to meet me."

"Oh, really? And I guess this isn't to discuss the newest round of test scores from the city's schools," I reply. "Get to the point, Joe. Sorry to rush you, but I've got a list of things to do."

"No offense taken. He offered me five million dollars to take you out," Joe says. "With a bonus the faster I get it done."

"And he knows you work for me, right?" I ask. "At least, the last time you were active in the city, it was for me."

"Of course he knows," Joe says. "But he still made the offer. Twice my normal rate for a hit of your . . . value."

"I'm honored. But if you're calling me, you didn't take the contract. That's not your style. So, what gives?" I ask, chilled by the idea of Joe Strauss after me. He's the sort of man deadlier than cancer. At least cancer can be beaten sometimes. "You're not the kind to switch sides, either."

"I know I'm not, which is something Jacob Waters doesn't seem to understand," Joe says. "I remember ideas like honor, Ryker. And I remember when you and your brother helped my daughter out with the problem she was having with those punks. Some things are more important than money, you know."

I nod, relieved. It wasn't much, just a bit of trouble that Joe couldn't get involved with directly, and I was more than willing to do him a favor. Seems my investment's reaping rewards. "I do know. Thank you, Joe."

"Don't mention it. Also, I wanted to pass on a little info. Waters is getting desperate. I don't know how far you're willing to push him, but I heard it in his voice—the man's close to cracking. If I were you, I'd end this soon before the streets run red with innocent blood. Trust me, you don't want that on your conscience."

"I plan on it. Thank you, Joe. Good night."

I hang up the phone, looking over at Marcus. "He's right, you know. Taking over the city's one thing, but I'm not the type to massacre the innocent."

Marcus nods, picking up his phone. "So how do you plan on doing it?"

I think, staring long and hard into the scarred, scratched surface of the table, running my fingers along the scratches and thinking about how familiar it feels. Sure, I might be living in a penthouse now, but the fact is that I've spent most of my life in grimy little offices like this. There have been so many nights sitting at a hand-me-down Formica table, so many nights where I wasn't wearing Gucci slacks but Dickies, my boots not custom-tailored but the Vietnam jungle variety. And if I'm going to end this quickly, I need to get back to the man I was.

"I need to get out on the streets, take it old school," I finally say. "Trade in the comfort for getting a little grit under my fingernails."

"Why?" Marcus asks. "Why not wait for him to come out? He's gotta come out eventually. If he sits on his ass, he's going to lose his rep."

"And if I sit on my ass, I'm going to lose the same thing," I reply. "I need to get my hands dirty again. You still got my old gear?"

Marcus nods. "The jacket, at least. Why, you want it?"

I think, then shake my head. "No, but I do need some street gear. What's here?"

"Enough that you'll find what you're looking for," Marcus says. "You sure about this, though?"

I nod, getting up. "Let me get changed. We'll talk while I do."

The lights are off when I open the door to Sarah's room, and I think she's sleeping at first, so I start to back out when her voice comes out of the darkness. "You're leaving."

"I need to. If I don't, this could stretch on for weeks,

even months. Innocent people could die. I signed up for this life, but most of this city didn't."

I close the door most of the way and cross over to Sarah's bed, kneeling next to her. She shifts and turns, rolling over to look at me, and in the darkness, her already dark eyes look nearly black, but still, I can see the emotion in them. It's hard to miss when she's nearly crying. "It's what makes you different from him," she says softly, reaching out and stroking my hair. "The only reason he'd even think of exposing himself would be to save his own neck."

"I know. And it's a weakness I'm going to exploit. I need to go stake him out, figure out where he's holed up," I reply. "I need to know where your husband is so I can position my troops and end this soon."

"Don't call him that," Sarah whispers fiercely. She takes her hand back, clasping her hands together for a moment before holding out her engagement and wedding rings for me. "I don't want them anymore. He has never been a husband to me."

I take them and tuck them into the left hip pocket on the baggy fatigue pants I'm wearing. It's been a long time, but they still feel right. "I'll toss them in the river."

"No," Sarah says. "I want you to keep them, because I don't want you to go. And I know you have to anyway. You have to bring those back to me so I can throw them in the river myself."

"You'll be safe here," I reassure her. "Unless it's a perfect opportunity, I won't make a move."

Sarah reaches out, cupping my face and kissing me again. "You'd better not. You come back, and I'll follow that up with every fantasy you've ever had of me."

I chuckle, getting to my feet and leaning over, giving her a little kiss on the nose. "I don't need the fantasy. The real thing was better than anything I ever fantasized. I'll see you in two to three days. At most."

CHAPTER 12

SARAH

*A*fter Ryker leaves, I try to stop my body from trembling, but I can't. After living in mortal fear for so long, I know it should be the opposite. When I was in that basement 'apartment', I was all alone. At night, when I shut off the games and tried to sleep, I couldn't hear anything except my own breathing. It scared me, thinking that I was all alone and that Jacob was coming for me. Now, I can hear people moving around in the 'safe house', and for some reason, it freaks me out. Finally, I can't take it anymore.

It's the fear that's getting to me, I know. *He's not coming back*, it says. He says he is, and he's got my rings that he's supposed to bring back to me once this is all over. But I can't stop this feeling that by this time tomorrow, Marcus is going to come in, telling me that Ryker's been shot in the streets and that I'm going to be turned over to Jacob as a last-ditch peace offering.

I'd rather die. So, now's my chance, and I take it, rolling out of bed just as the door opens. I freeze until I see that it's Marcus. "Sorry, didn't mean to wake you."

"It's okay. I was just getting up to use the bathroom, wherever that is," I reply. "What's up?"

He holds up a pair of shoes and socks. "These might be better for you than the sandals. The bathroom's over in the corner by the stairs to your right as you come out of the office."

"Thank you. And Marcus?" I reply, taking the shoes from him. They're not much, cheap Velcro-closed, bargain basement running shoes, but I appreciate the thought behind it. "Thank you."

"No problem," Marcus says, waiting while I slip the shoes on and get up. "This place ain't much, but we'll keep you warm, dry, and safe, at least."

We cross the warehouse, which is creepily empty. The fluorescents above me buzz slightly, casting a pale glare that leaves me feeling even more desperate, more worried. "Where is everyone?"

"Ryker taught us that you don't defend by huddling up but by doing what's called 'active defense', or going out and making sure your enemy never even gets close," Marcus says. "So, I'm the only one inside the building, acting as a sort of headquarters and communications center while the rest of the crew's out and around the neighborhood."

We reach the bathroom, which is by a door, and my fear flares out of control. "Okay, I'll wait here while you—"

He never completes his sentence as I turn and knee him square in the balls. He's not expecting it, and I catch him hard, knocking him to the ground with the pain. "Sorry, Marcus."

I run out the door, down the alley, and into the night. Rounding the corner, I try to remember what I saw through the front window of the van that we used to get here, and I think that the freeway is about two miles or so to my left. I take off in that direction, trying to look cool and collected while still hurrying.

My heart pounds in my chest as I make my way along the dimly lit alleys, doing my best to try and stay in a more or less straight line. Fear assaults me in every direction. Everybody I see moving in the streetlights could be a threat. I'm not from here. I wasn't born in the gritty parts of town. I've never learned how to fight for my next meal or what to look out for. I can't tell if someone's looking at me warily or if they mean me harm. I'm just a suburban girl who, long ago, thought about being an actress before getting caught up in a nightmare. I don't get far when someone jumps out and drags me into an alley, a powerful hand clamping over my mouth. "What the fuck are you doing?"

The voice in my ear immediately makes me stop fighting, and he lets me go. I turn to see Ryker, his eyes blazing with anger in the streetlight. "Ryker!"

His hands tighten on my arms, and he looks around before dragging me toward an apartment building, shoving me inside one of the first-floor apartments. There's a girl there who doesn't look as surprised as she should be when Ryker brings me in. I don't know who she is or why I'm feeling it, but I can't help but feel a surge of jealousy. "Go tell Marcus I found her. Tell him I'll bring her back in a little bit."

"I ain't got a phone, Ryker," the girl says, throwing up her hands when Ryker gives her a glare that could melt steel. "Fine. I'll walk over."

The girl gets up and disappears. Ryker doesn't say a word until she leaves, and then he turns to me, his eyes still blazing. "Now . . . what the fuck were you doing?"

"Ryker, I'm sorry. Please, I heard what you told Marcus. Jacob's hiring hitmen to try and get you. I had to get away. There's no way you can fight his money and power. I just . . . I want to live again!" I babble. I'm sure I'm repeating myself, and tears are flowing down my face as Ryker takes me in his arms and kisses me again, a habit for shutting me up that I'm quickly finding I'm not all that opposed to.

"I'm not letting you free just yet," Ryker says. "Sarah, you don't know this city. You were just about to cross over from my territory to an area controlled by a group still affiliated with Jacob."

"Ryker, just call Jacob. Say you killed me or something.

He won't care. He's still going to want to fight, and I can—"

"No," Ryker says, his tone cutting me off. "You will have a future, Sarah. When I kill him. Then you can go wherever you want. You'll be rich, even."

"What are you talking about?" I ask, and Ryker chuckles.

"Who do you think gets his estate when I kill him?" Ryker asks. "You can go anywhere you want. Be anything you want. You'll be free. Even if the fucker didn't leave it to you, I'll make sure it happens."

I shouldn't believe him. He's a criminal too, and other than giving me little bits of freedom and the best fuck of my life, I've been just as much his prisoner as I ever was with Jacob. But . . . looking up into his eyes, I want to believe him. "Promise?"

Ryker nods. "Promise. And if you'll let me, I'd like to take your pain away."

There's something in his eyes that says he's telling me the truth, and when he leans in to kiss me, I kiss him back, wrapping my arms around his neck and tasting his honesty in his lips and his tongue.

We pull at each other's clothes, making our way to the couch, where Ryker pulls me on top of him, straddling his waist while his lips make their way down my throat and over my collarbones. I tense at first when his hands trace my scar again, but then the warmth of his touch seeps through the self-consciousness, and I look down into his face, stroking his hair. "When I'm with you, I'm not afraid."

"And you'll never have to be," Ryker says, raising his head. His tongue traces over my skin, the touch making me forget all my worries. I feel his cock swell and stiffen underneath me, and I start riding him, rubbing my still panty-covered mound against the thick bulge in his pants. "Mmm, slowly, beautiful."

"Say it again," I gasp, pulling his head against my chest as his tongue circles around my right nipple, teasing me and sending fireworks through me. "Please, Ryker, say it again."

"Beautiful," he murmurs before he wraps his lips around my nipple and sucks, making me gasp and cry out softly. We're on a ratty old sofa in a flea trap of an apartment, but I don't care. This is better than any luxury setting as Ryker's hands and lips weave patterns of pleasure and heat over my body. Grinding against him, my pussy is soaked, and I let myself be swept away in his arms, standing up just long enough to let him slide my panties off. He's sitting in front of me, and I feel vulnerable but somehow safe as he leans forward and kisses my belly button, making me giggle. "Ticklish?"

"A little," I tease, running my fingers through his hair. "Why did fate make me waste years with him?"

"It doesn't matter," Ryker says, leaning in again and kissing my waist. "We have now."

Heated trepidation sweeps through me as Ryker gets off the couch, kneeling on the floor to give himself better access as I naturally spread my legs. His lips travel lower and lower until I can feel his breath on my pussy lips and his hands holding my ass tenderly. His tongue caresses my pussy, and it's like heaven, sliding through my slick folds, nibbling and lapping at me, tasting me and swallowing me with eager sounds of pleasure. It's so good that I have to put my hands on his shoulders just to keep myself from falling over. But Ryker's strong arms give me a sort of saddle to sit in as he devours me, and I relax into them, letting myself get washed away in the sensations.

Ryker's tongue flickers over my clit and I cry out, tears of ecstasy rolling down my cheeks as untold new pleasure rolls through my body and I grind against his eager lips and tongue, Ryker not stopping until I'm trembling on the edge of coming. With a single lick, he shatters me, my body carried away as my knees unlock and I sink down. He lowers me slowly, and I feel the heat of his cock pressing against the entrance to my pussy.

Ryker twists us so that he can lie back on the carpet while I sink down onto him. There's none of the pain of being stretched open like last time, just one glorious feeling of being filled, of being joined with someone who wants me as me. "And that . . . fuck, you're perfect."

I ride him, his words giving me even more encouragement, sliding my hips back and forth and letting his cock fill me again and again. I want to go slow, but after coming so hard from his tongue, I'm greedy, voracious for more of Ryker, and my hips take over, riding him hard and fast, squeezing him and dangling my breasts over his face. He's more than happy to feast on me, his lips finding my left nipple and sucking hard, devouring me and sending my brain whirling.

It's forever and it's an instant, the feeling of his cock sliding in and out of me making time simultaneously stand still and whip past us at hurricane speeds. Still, I've never felt better than I do in Ryker's arms, and another orgasm builds within me, this one bigger but more tender, it seems. "Ryker, help me."

He plants his feet, his hips jackhammering upward, driving his long, thick cock into my pussy as I find his lips again and we kiss, both of us moaning as the feelings wash over us. His fingers dig into the soft flesh of my ass as he reaches his climax, and he's moaning, his cock erupting deep inside me and pushing me over the edge, my own orgasm filling my body with not just pleasure but the warm light of something that I've never felt before. When it passes, I stay on top of him. I want to draw out this moment of perfection as long as possible.

"Thank you," I whisper, kissing him again. "For making me a woman again."

"I swear I will make sure you're protected," Ryker says, looking up into my eyes. "I only wish—"

The door to the apartment bursts open, and both of us turn to see Marcus with about four other men and the girl from the apartment. Marcus's eyes open wide, and he turns quickly, but not before a couple of people in the hallway see us. "Oh, shit! Sorry!"

The door closes, and I can't help it, the ridiculousness of the whole thing makes me laugh. "Sorry?"

"He's my brother. What am I going to do?" Ryker asks, looking over at the clock. "Oh, that's why."

"Why?" I ask, then look over at the clock. "Fuck, how long were we . . .?"

"About an hour and a half. He probably got antsy, thought maybe we got in trouble. Come on, let's get dressed," Ryker says, pausing to give me a deep look. I slip off him and get dressed as quickly as I can while he pulls his shirt back on and adjusts his pants. When Marcus knocks softly a minute later, we're decent, and Ryker opens the door, looking at his brother and the girl from the apartment, who's wearing a bemused and outraged expression on her face. "Sorry to worry you guys."

"Oh, sure, just use my place as a love nest," the girl says

in a saucy accent. "You'd better not have left any stains!"

"Shut up, Tiffany," Marcus says. "You'll get what's coming to you."

Out in the street, the other men look at me differently, but then again, I guess you always look at a woman differently after you've seen her naked and impaled on a cock. Ryker ignores them though, talking to his brother. "Take Sarah back to the safe house, and you stay by her side until I get back."

"I got it," Marcus says, as the two brothers embrace. "You sure about this?"

"Damn sure," Ryker says. "It ends tonight."

Ryker turns to walk away, and I go to call him but realize he doesn't need the distraction. Suddenly, he stops and turns, coming over to me and kissing me, pulling me into his arms and holding me close before letting me go, cupping my chin again. "For luck. I'll see you when I get back."

He turns and rushes off into the darkness, and I watch him for as long as possible before Marcus puts a gentle hand on my shoulder. "Come on. These streets aren't safe right now."

"Hey," I ask, my lips still tingling from Ryker's passionate kiss. It's his promise, and I am going to hold onto that promise as long as I can. "What did you mean to that girl, that she'd get what's coming?"

Marcus stops, then chuckles. "Guess that did sound rough, didn't it? I meant we'd pay her rent on that place for the month. It's Ryker's style. We use your stuff, we compensate you. It's how we were able to get so much loyalty in only five years. Treat the people right, and they support us."

CHAPTER 13

RYKER

*E*verything I've studied and practiced and done over the past five years is telling me that what I'm doing is stupid. That I need to take a few days to let him sweat, to make him start to relax his guard. Maybe even to let a little paranoia set in. Or that maybe I should've just taken Jacob out from day one.

The call came in from a trusted source, but that doesn't mean much. Trust in my world only goes so far except in cases of people like Marcus. As the old saying goes, for most men, at least, everyone's got a price. And Waters still has plenty of money to throw around. For all I know, Jacob could be sitting at his house, chilling out with a crew of a dozen men just waiting for me to show up.

So I should be doing anything other than what I'm doing, which is crawling up the slope that surrounds

Waters's mansion alone. For fuck's sake, I don't even have any guns with me, just a pair of double-edged fighting knives. I should be hitting this house with every fucking thing I've got. Instead, I'm crawling up this slope like some ninja out of the movies. And why? First, because I want to feel Jacob Waters's blood on my hands, and a pistol's too quick for him. Secondly, and more practically, because if I shoot, that's going to bring every single man Jacob's got in the area right on top of me. If I want to make it back to Sarah, I need to do this quietly.

I slide up another two feet, pausing to listen whether I've been detected. The silence doesn't reassure me, but I can't let my fear get in the way. I check my watch. I've been crawling up this slope for nearly an hour, and it's getting close to three in the morning. It's the ideal time for this crazy fucking idea of mine, the time when any guards are going to be sleepy and everyone should be more or less not alert.

I crest the slope and get behind the brick retaining wall that forms the outer edge of the lawn at the Waters estate, looking carefully through the gaps in the design. There's no movement, none, but I keep watch. If I am going to survive this, not only is my reputation assured, but this is going to be over. On the other hand, if I'm going to survive this, I need to be smart.

I watch for ten minutes, looking for any sign of move-ment at all, and there's none. Still, the last report

Marcus fed to me said that Jacob Waters was sighted going into his mansion around midnight and his driver pulled away twenty minutes later.

I cross the lawn and go to the back door, trying it and finding it locked. Not a problem. I didn't get to where I am without learning a few things about breaking and entering, and this door's a piece of cake. Jacob's always had a reputation that matters more than any lock for keeping his house secure.

Creeping through the dark house is weird. I keep wondering if this room or that was a place where Jacob did terrible things to Sarah. The feeling only increases when I see a dark shape laid out on the floor in the dining room. I approach carefully, kneeling and turning on a pen light, horrified when the blank, dead eyes of a blonde girl look back up at me, her face a puffy wreck and her throat cut ear to ear. "Sweet Jesus."

"She tried to say no," a now familiar voice says behind me. I turn, staying low as Jacob Waters comes in, a short samurai sword in his right hand, the edge dark with what I know is this girl's blood. He's limping a little from where Marcus shot him in the ass, but not all that much. "Nobody says no to me."

"Didn't think you'd be up," I comment, trying to buy time. "Night owl?"

"Something like that," Jacob says, swinging the sword. I may be half his age, but he's got a fucking razor-sharp sword and he's fast. I barely roll out of the way of the first blow, gaining a little distance and getting to my feet, pulling both of my knives, reversing the one in my left hand to protect myself.

"Nice knives," Jacob says, adjusting his grip and taking a trained stance. I hope it's just something he saw in movies. I mean, who the fuck studies sword fighting nowadays? "I have a similar pair in my study."

"Why not go get them, make this even?" I grunt, keeping my eyes not on the glittering tip of the sword but his wrists. It's one of the first lessons I learned about how to fight with a blade. Where the wrists go, the blade follows, so keep your eyes there. "Then again, you're the kind who doesn't play fair."

"Says the guy who stole my wife and tries to use her as a human shield," Waters says, thrusting his sword forward on the final word. I see it coming and duck, stepping forward and slicing the side and back of his right leg before momentum carries us apart again, Waters groaning in pain and starting to limp some more. "I'll have your head on my desk!"

Waters doesn't give me a chance to reply, swinging his blade in small X shapes that force me to retreat out of the dining room and into the hallway. Here, I can't go around his blade, and I back up more, trying to draw him into another big space. "You're not a man, Jacob. You're not even an animal."

"What the fuck do I care?" Waters asks, grinning. "So long as they fear me."

"They're going to fear *me* in the future," I reply, stepping into what feels like the main foyer of the house. It's huge, with a marble staircase that curves up and around, and I know I must end this here. I can't bet on having enough space to fight him anywhere else. "Just like she's going to be mine after this."

"She's mine," Waters says, his breath coming in shallow gasps. Maybe I hit a vein, or maybe he's just not in very good shape, but he's tired already, the tip of his sword wavering in the dim moonlight coming through the windows.

"Huh. She called out my name a lot over the past few days," I taunt, trying to provoke him into a berserker rage. I want him sloppy. I can't get past that sword without it. "Then again, she did say you're a little . . . short in certain areas."

Waters roars, raising his sword over his head, and I take my chance, stepping in and slicing upward with my right hand, cutting him across both wrists deeply, his sword falling from his now useless hands to clatter to the marble. Meanwhile, my left hand brings my knife up to press into his throat. Waters tries to jerk his head back, but not in time as I draw my blade across, a fountain of blood erupting out to cover my arm and face. He sinks to his knees, staring up at me with rage and a total lack of understanding in his eyes.

"If I were going for justice, I'd shoot you in the head right now like you shot my father," I say, kicking him in the chest. He falls back, still trying to breathe as the blood flows from his neck to shine black in the moonlight. Appropriate for someone whom I just said wasn't even human. I squat down, staring into his fading eyes, where panic and a glimmer of understanding are starting to emerge. "But I'm not a very just man."

I watch for another minute as Jacob Waters bleeds out, his blood pooling underneath him on the marble flooring. When he twitches his last, I cut a piece from his shirt and dip it in the blood, writing my message on the tile. *The King is dead. Long live the King of the Streets.*

Satisfied, I walk out, leaving the door open and exposing Jacob's body to the elements. I'm halfway down the hill when a car pulls up and someone gets out. "Jesus! What the hell happened to you?"

It's one of Waters's men, but my face is so covered in blood that he doesn't recognize me until I get closer, and by then, it's too late as I jack him against the car, my knife at his throat. "There are two bodies up there. One of them is my work. The other was that fucker's work. Put the word out. I'm the man in town now. I'm the new king."

The man nods shallowly, and I take my knife away long enough to let him start to relax before I grab his head and slam it into the roof of his car, knocking him out. His body drops to the pavement, and I check his pulse to make sure he's okay.

Having a witness like this makes things easier in some ways.

Still, kinda sucks to not take his car. It's a pretty long walk.

CHAPTER 14

For the first time, the warehouse feels crowded as nearly a dozen people sit around the office and outside in the main room, tiredly shooting the shit. They just got off shift protecting the neighborhood and protecting me, and while I should feel grateful to these ten men and two women, all I can think of is Ryker.

I feel like an outsider. These people grew up in housing projects nearby, learning in the streets. They grew up fighting, and while trying to become a teen actress wasn't exactly all fun and games, they've had a harder life than I've had.

Even their language is different. When they throw around the street slang that the scriptwriters used to get me to try occasionally, they sound comfortable with it. They know exactly how to use it, what it means. They don't look like they're going to stumble over their own tongues, forcing the words out and trying not to giggle like I used to.

Still, the conversation is quiet, and as Marcus takes a seat next to me, he hands me a cup of coffee. "You know, you don't need to be up yet. For sure, you don't need to be sitting around here with us deplorable types."

"Kinda lonely lying on the bed, and I couldn't get back to sleep," I whisper, looking down. I don't know why I should be so emotional, but I am. After sleeping fitfully for only a few hours, I decided to get up. "They keep looking at me . . ."

"It's been a while," Marcus says simply, sipping his coffee. "A lot of the crew is wondering about you."

"About what?" I ask, and one of the other people laughs.

"We're wondering if you really are Rygirl or not," someone jokes, earning a few chuckles before an icy stare from Marcus shuts him up and people start to leave the office area. "Fuck, man, just making a joke."

"Would you say that if Ryker were here?" Marcus asks, and the man shakes his head. "Then get the fuck out."

The man closes the door behind him, and Marcus sits down, shaking his head in frustration. I'm totally confused, and I look at him. "Rygirl?"

Marcus nods. "It's just a stupid term the crew came up with for when he found a real girlfriend, not a part-time fling. For most of the time that Ryker's been in charge of our gang, he's been single. Our lives sort of demand it outside of what you can guess. Oh, by the way, sorry about walking in on you guys earlier."

"It's okay. You were concerned about your brother," I reply, reaching out and patting him on the shoulder. "You know, for all the tough guy act you show the crew, you're pretty sensitive."

Marcus chuckles, shrugging. "Maybe. I do know that I hope you are Rygirl. He needs someone in his life besides me."

"Ryker's Girl?" I ask as I make the connection, and Marcus nods. "But I'm not his girl! I mean, sure, you saw us, well . . ."

"I saw," Marcus says. "And I'm man enough to admit that I was a little jealous of Ryker. Back when we were kids and you were on TV, I was the one with the bigger crush on you than him. I actually wrote you a fan letter once, although all I got back was a form letter from your talent agency."

I chuckle, nodding. It helps, Marcus's admission, helping me recenter a little. "At one point, I was getting ten thousand letters a week. Now I get none. To be honest, I prefer getting none. But still, just because the two of us were . . . together, that doesn't make me his girl."

"No, it doesn't," Marcus agrees. "But when he turned around to give you that kiss before he left, that's all I needed to see. Everyone knows it. Except for maybe you, it seems."

"It's only been a few days, Marcus. Maybe a little over a week?"

He shrugs. "When you know what you want, you know what you want. Ryker's always been like that. Either way, he's been different and I like the new Ryker I'm seeing this past week. More heart, less cold-blooded. Tell you one thing—he needs more than me in his life."

I nod, looking down. "Still, it's not like that."

"You never know. Like I said, Ryker doesn't fuck around," Marcus says. "And you two have chemistry. I saw that back at the penthouse. The way you'd talk about him when I was keeping you company, the way he talked about you . . . I could tell something was happening."

"Can we change the subject?" I ask finally, and he hums, shrugging. "Uh, if I can ask, you've talked about your father. What about your mother?"

Marcus finishes his coffee, sighing. "Took off when Ryker and I were still in junior high. Pop was dedicated to the life. The gang came first, and she couldn't deal with that no more. Last I heard, she met a guy out west and got remarried. By now, she might even have another kid or two."

"That's gotta be tough," I say, and Marcus shrugs again. There's a defeated tone to that shrug that makes me sad. It's like Marcus understands that it's wrong for a man to not make his wife and his family the most important things in his life, but that's the way gang life is. It sucks, but there's nothing that can be done about it. It scares me and saddens me that Ryker might feel the same.

Finally, Marcus gets up, pouring himself another cup of coffee before he sits down and speaks again. "It is what it is. I understand why she did it. I don't have any hate for her or anything like that. For Pop, the gang was number one, and that has to suck for any woman, whether that number one is a business, a gang, the army, whatever. I used to wonder what my life would have been like if Mom had taken Ryker and me with her, but it don't matter now."

There's a rising murmur of sound outside the meeting room, and Marcus looks up, a smile coming to his face. "He's back."

I turn, getting to my feet just as I see him cross the warehouse, blood all over him. "Ryker!"

Marcus hears something in my tone of voice and laughs. "Sure seems like you're Rygirl to me."

"It's not like that!" I yell, but Marcus's grin never wavers.

The door opens, and Ryker comes closer, his face and body exhausted, but his eyes sparkle when he sees me. "What's not like that?"

There's a crowd gathering outside, everyone almost silently respectful as Ryker leans against the door frame and Marcus gets a chair for his brother. "Nothing, brother," Marcus says. "We're just glad to have you back, that's all."

I can feel the heat rise to my cheeks as I sit back down, and Ryker comes over, pulling out the chair and sitting next to me. A few of the idiots outside mutter, but it dies as soon as Ryker glares back over his shoulder. He turns back to me, his eyes softening as he puts a comforting hand on my leg.

The fact is, I don't know what to think. Feeling his hand on my thigh, I feel something I've never felt before. It damn sure isn't at all like Jacob's charm when he was dating me and I didn't know that the charismatic smile hid a monster on the other side.

Ryker is different. As his hand rests on my thigh, he's not demanding and he's not saying he understands. Just that . . . it feels like he accepts me. Finally, I look up at him, swallowing the lump in my throat as I take in the blackened blood that's covered half his face. "Is he . . .?"

Ryker nods. "By my hand."

"Was there anyone else home?" I ask, and Ryker nods, the look in his eyes sending a chill down my spine. "Oh, no . . . Stanzie?"

"A blonde girl. She was dead when I arrived," Ryker says. "I'd have called when it was done, but I broke my damn phone in the fight, and then I had to get other things done. Marcus . . .?"

Ryker's words hit me hard, and I think about poor, sweet Stanzie, who never had a chance. If there's anything that I can do for her, I swear to myself, I'm going to do it. She had a piss-poor life that I couldn't do anything about, but she's going to be honored in her death, that I can swear.

All of this flashes through my mind in the heartbeat after Ryker's question. Marcus's phone rings before he can answer, though, and he pulls it out, listening quickly before saying one phrase in reply. "Yeah, we'll call you back."

He turns to Ryker, his eyes looking at his brother in wonder. "That was a contact from the mayor's office. They want to meet."

Ryker nods, leaning back in exhaustion. "Then it's done. Marcus, get a car. I want to go home."

I have to help Ryker from the elevator to the bedroom when we get up to the penthouse, shaking my head when Marcus offers his hand. "Okay," Marcus says. "I'll make sure this building's on lockdown. You'll have plenty of people downstairs just in case. No worries for the next few hours."

"Thank you," I tell Marcus. "Marcus . . ."

"Don't worry, just take care of him."

Marcus leaves, and I turn, going over to the bed, where Ryker's lying stretched out, his right arm over his face and his chest heaving. I close the bedroom door and sit down next to him, laying a hand over his heart. "You okay?"

Ryker takes his arm away from his eyes and looks at me in the soft light filtering through the shaded windows, swallowing. "I . . . I watched him die, Sarah. I thought I'd feel different about it."

"How do you feel?" I ask, feeling his heart hammering in his body.

"Good . . . and hollow," he says. "I did what needed to be done. Not for vengeance—that's what I feel hollow about—but for you. I'm glad I killed him."

"So am I," I whisper. I lean down, softly kissing him on the lips before tracing his lips with my tongue. Ryker stirs at my caress, his hands coming up to pull me down onto his body, kissing me back.

"You know you don't have to," he says when we pause for breath.

I smile, stroking his face as I straddle his hips and run my fingers through his hair. "I don't, which is what makes you so wonderful. But Ryker, you've won your prize. Now take what's yours."

He looks up, the exhaustion dropping in an instant from his face as my words make an impact. He reaches up, pulling me down onto him and kissing me hard. My breasts smash against his chest as he reaches down, crushing me to him and grabbing my ass, massaging it and setting my pussy on fire with need.

"Yes." I groan as Ryker's hand slides inside my sweatpants and strokes my skin. Pushing away, I pull my shirt off, rolling off him to lie on my back, submitting to him completely.

Ryker gets to his knees, tearing his shirt off and getting off the bed long enough to push his pants down, stepping out of his boots. "Strip for me, Sarah. Now."

His command is like nothing that Jacob ever did. I feel sexy and powerful as I push my sweatpants down, playfully kicking them off before lifting my hips and pushing down my panties. When they're off, I spread my legs for Ryker, holding my knees apart. "Do you really think I'm desirable?"

Ryker's eyes tear themselves from my wet pussy to look me in the eye, and in his gaze, I see something that I thought didn't exist any longer. He wants me, but at the same time . . . he respects me. He wants more than just to fuck me and prove his manly dominance. A lot more.

"I think you're the most beautiful woman in the world," Ryker says, climbing onto the bed and taking ahold of my left ankle. He adjusts my legs so that he's in between, his cock standing out thick and hard from between his legs as he climbs higher. The whole time, he never breaks eye contact with me, but instead, he slips his hands behind my knees, slowly curling me up until the thick root of his cock brushes against my pussy lips, resting there and sending trembles through my body. "I think you're an angel."

Ryker starts thrusting his cock slowly, leaning down and kissing me and letting our tongues twist and tangle around each other as his cockhead rubs between my lips and over the head of my clit. I wrap my legs around him, hopelessly unable to resist him as my body is thrilled with every slow thrust, wetness coating Ryker until, with a stretching sensation that I never want to forget, he fills me with one long, deep thrust of his cock.

"God, you're fucking perfect," I hiss as he grinds against me, stretching me and electrifying nerves that still are not too sure they even exist. "Ryker, one request?"

"What's that?" he asks, putting his hands on the mattress on each side of my head and looking down at me as he pins me down. "Am I going too hard?"

I smile and reach up, cupping the back of his head. "No. Not every time, but . . . give it to me as hard as you want. Right now, I'm a hundred percent yours, and I want you to take me that way."

Ryker nods, a smirk coming to his sexy lips as he pulls back, pausing at my entrance. "Just remember, you asked for it. And if it's too much, just say 'please.'"

Before I can reply, he thrusts hard, my eyes flying open

as his hips smack against my ass and my pussy feels like a pleasure explosion's gone off inside it. I let go of Ryker's neck to claw at his shoulders, holding on for dear life as he pounds my body with abandon.

It's . . . there are no words to describe how it feels. I never thought I could let myself be put into a position of being like this again. Ryker risked his life to gain my freedom, and tonight, I give it to him, and he's *rewarding* me by giving me the absolute most mind-blowing fuck of my life.

I wrap my legs around him tightly, trying to squeeze and give as good as I'm getting, but it's no use. Ryker's a force of nature, thrilling me with every stroke of his cock, every inch of my skin tingling as his hard chest muscles rub against my nipples and our flesh seems to become nothing but an unending connection.

Time slips away again, carried away in the tide of our panting breath, the sweat coating our skin and making everything both slicker and more on fire. Ryker captures my mouth in another intense kiss before licking my ear and nipping at it with his teeth. "Nobody . . . nobody better than you."

His words trigger my release, and I moan, digging in my fingernails as I come hard, pulling him deep into me. Ryker shudders, his cock swelling before he comes too, the feeling of his heat inside me drawing out the moment and making it feel like it'll last forever.

Of course, it can't, but as we collapse, lying next to each

other, Ryker pulls me close, letting me rest my head on his chest. I feel both of us start to drift off, and that's fine. I'm sure if anything needs to happen, Marcus will wake us.

"Thank you," Ryker mumbles sleepily just as the gray curtain of sleep fogs my brain. "Thank you for giving me a few days of what I've always wanted. I only wish . . ."

I don't hear anymore as sleep pulls me the rest of the way down, taking with it my reply.

CHAPTER 15

*T*he streets glitter in diamond lights below me as the last of the sun disappears below the horizon. I look down at it, surveying my kingdom. I'm the King of the City now. The meeting with the mayor this afternoon, just the two of us, with no press, no retainers, just two guys having a couple of muffins in the park, cemented my status.

I have the keys to the city. I'm the king, and everyone knows it. Nobody's going to come after me for Jacob's death, not until they think they can gain an advantage. No one loved him. They only feared him.

I hear the click of high heels behind me, and I turn, momentarily stunned as Sarah comes into the living room, looking for the first time like the Hollywood starlet she used to be. I'd told Marcus to make sure she was outfitted properly for whatever she wants to do, and as usual, my brother came through. "You look . . . amazing."

Sarah blushes slightly, tucking a long strand of her lustrous black hair behind her ear and smiling a little. "You look a lot better after a shower, a shave, and a nap too. I–I wanted to wait until you were free before I said goodbye."

I look behind her, and I see that she's got a small backpack already, her few things there with the ridiculous shoes Marcus got her sticking out of the top. Sarah looks over her shoulder, seeing what I'm looking at and laughing slightly. "Yeah, I decided to keep them. They're really comfortable. And they'll remind me of this."

"Where will you go?" I ask huskily, my throat not wanting to work. "Back to Hollywood?"

Sarah shakes her head, looking down. "No. Let's face it —that part of my life ended a long time ago."

I nod, not sure what to say. "So . . .?"

"I thought maybe I'd take the money that's now in *my* accounts and go to the beach for a while. It's been five years since I left this city on my own, and well . . . it'd help."

I swallow, stepping forward. "The beach sounds nice."

Sarah nods, looking at me with confusion for a little bit before she steps forward and puts her hands on my shoulders. "Thank you, Ryker. You probably saved my life. You definitely gave me a chance at a real life."

In her heels, we're the same height, and when she kisses me, I feel something inside me loosen, something that I've kept under wraps for too long. When she goes to step away, I grab her wrist, not hard, but still enough to stop her. She whips her head back, her hair flying over her shoulder as she looks at me with those beautiful dark eyes as they widen in shock and maybe . . . hope?

"I don't want you to go," I say. "I want you to stay."

I let go of her wrist, and she turns, her face twisting in a rich play of emotions as fear, desire, and I don't know what else runs through her. "Ryker, you promised me that when you'd killed Jacob, I could go free."

I nod, reaching out more tentatively and taking her hand. "I did. And you deserve your freedom more than anyone in the whole fucking world. And I will keep my word. You can leave if you want, but I want you, Sarah."

"As your prisoner?" she asks, and I shake my head, stepping forward and putting my hand around her waist, pulling her to me.

"No. Next to me. Every king needs his queen."

Sarah puts her hands on my chest, pushing away gently. "Ryker, I . . . I want you too. But I can't be number two. I won't do to you what Marcus said your mother did."

At this moment, I could damn near kill my brother, but he's right, and Sarah's right too. She can't be number two. I'm the king, and my kingdom deserves a king who is focused on it first. I pause, and Sarah steps back, going to her bag and picking it up. "Goodbye, Ryker."

She steps into the elevator, and as the doors close, I know what I need to do. I run as hard as I can for the stairs, pulling my new phone out of my pocket as I pelt down the stairs. "Marcus!"

"What do you need?" Marcus asks. "I'm at the club, enjoying some drinks. Thought we were taking the night off?"

"Get over here. I need to talk to you. Now!" I say, hanging up before he can reply. I put my phone in my pocket, pausing at the thirty-third floor and praying that the taxi is slow in coming to pick Sarah up.

I'm gasping for breath by the time I hit the latch bar on the door and emerge into the building's foyer. Even though I'm going down, running down forty-eight flights of stairs on a dead sprint is fucking hard. I cross the space, running out into the parking lot just as the taxi starts to pull away. "SARAH!"

The taxi stops, and I run up, pulling open the door. She's sitting there, her eyes wide, and the taxi driver is looking over his shoulder at me like I'm a psycho. Hell, maybe at this moment, I am, but I know what needs to be done. "Ryker?"

I reach in, taking her by the hand and helping her out of the car before I pull her into a hug. "Sarah, stay. Not as number two but as number one. I don't want this fucking city."

Sarah's shocked, looking into my eyes as my words sink in. "You mean . . .?"

"Give me twenty minutes. You can sit in when Marcus gets here. I promise you, it'll change both of our lives."

Sarah nods, closing the door on the cab. The taxi driver honks his horn, looking out his window. "Hey, lady, you going to the airport or what?"

Sarah turns, shaking her head. "Sorry, no. Sorry to have wasted your time."

The driver looks like he's about to bitch about it when he finally recognizes me, and before he can get worried, I pull my money clip out of my pocket and peel off two one hundred dollar bills, handing them through the window to him. "A tip, for your excellent service. Have a good evening."

"You're fucking nuts," Marcus says, looking at me and Sarah in shock as he takes in what I just repeated to him for the third time. "You don't want to be king?"

"No," I reply, holding Sarah's hand. "Some things are more important than money and power."

"And you want me to take over? Ryker, I'm not the brains of this operation. You know that—" Marcus says, and I hold up a hand, stopping him.

"You've got plenty of brains, Marcus. And I'm not abandoning you. I'm just saying that . . . well, let the city think that I'm still the king for a while if you want. I don't give a fuck. But the day-to-day operations, the real power, that's you. I'll still be around for advice if you really need it. Face it, though, Marcus—you've been running a lot of it by yourself for a while. Half the time I ask for things, you've already done them."

He shakes his head, looking down. "You're fucking nuts."

"You keep saying that," Sarah says with a chuckle. "To quote from my previous life, I do not think it means what you think it means."

Marcus looks at Sarah, then chuckles. "I'm even more jealous of you now, Ryker. Got the crown, got the girl, and now you're just giving up the crown because the girl's more important. All right, man, if that's what you want. Can you gimme six months to work a smooth transition? Like you, I don't want a crime war in this city."

I look at Sarah, who nods, and I offer Marcus my hand. "Six months. Minus this next week. I'm taking Sarah on vacation tomorrow. Then yeah, I'll give you six months of help."

Marcus takes my hand, shaking it. "Okay, then. Well, I guess my night out just became more of a celebration for myself. I'll give you two your privacy. I already figured on staying out all night. Oh, and I'll start looking for my own place. No offense, but you two . . . you're gonna need your own digs." Marcus gets up and leaves, giving us both a laugh and a wave as he gets in the elevator. "Good job, Rygirl!"

The doors close, and Sarah laughs, turning and putting her arms around my neck. "You realize Marcus is right? You just gave up an entire kingdom."

"And gained something far more valuable," I reply, putting my hands on her waist. "I'm not saying it's going to be perfect. I can't cook for shit, although maybe now, I've got the spare time to learn how. And I know it's not guaranteed between us, but I know when I want something, and I want you."

Sarah grins, leaning in to whisper in my ear. "So, Ryker Johns, how about you take me to your bed, and we celebrate your losing your throne?"

I growl, picking her up in my arms and carrying her toward my bedroom. "Well then, I suppose we'll just have to go shopping for a new set of lingerie before we go on vacation, because I might just tear them off you."

Sarah chuckles, wrapping her legs around my waist as

we make our way down the hallway toward my bedroom. "My King."

I kiss her and lay her on my bed, looking into her beautiful eyes. "My Queen."

And that's all I fucking need.

CHAPTER 16

The sun barely peeks through the wall of windows in my penthouse bedroom, but it's enough to rouse me from sleep. Okay, so it's not just the sun. After a long night of 'work', I've gotten used to sleeping until the sun's high in the sky. Maybe my early awakening is because of the beautiful form in my arms, wiggling around softly and pressing her ass against my quickly hardening cock. I chuckle, kissing the back of her neck as I pull her closer, pressing my hips forward and running my hand over her stomach. "Mmm, you are wonderful to wake up to."

Sarah hums, sighing and half gasping as she parts her legs and lets my cock slip between them, not inside yet, but we both know that's what we want. "Good morning. Is this something you're going to tell me every morning?"

"Well, it's more true than ever," I murmur, inhaling her

intoxicating scent. "You make my life as close to perfect as I could imagine. Better, actually. Not that I ever imagined that avenging my father's murder would lead me to fall in love with the most beautiful woman in the world."

"Please." Sarah chuckles, sighing happily as she squeezes her thighs around my cock and I slowly start thrusting over her pussy lips. "I'm just a washed-up teenage fantasy."

"You," I counter, bringing my hand up to cup her breast and rub my thumb over her nipple, making it become diamond-hard before I roll it between my forefinger and thumb, "are far from a washed-up teenage fantasy."

Sarah moans again, and I can feel her wetness coating the shaft of my cock. We haven't exactly been 'safe', but that's sort of been the speed and intensity of our relationship. Before, I was too caught up in the whirlwind of everything going on to think about it. Now, the idea that there may be consequences is even more exciting.

"I admit, you make me feel special. I mean, you gave up your kingdom for me."

"Without you, it wasn't worth it anyway," I whisper, stroking her breast just the way she likes. "So I did, and here we are."

I lift my head to peek at the clock, silently celebrating that it's so early because we definitely have time for some morning action before I meet Marcus for breakfast. I pull my cock from between her legs, rolling onto my back and pulling Sarah on top of me. It's one of the things I've learned quickly with her. She's got more than just physical scars, and in the morning, it's good to let her be on top.

Sarah grins from on top of me before glancing at the clock and seeing the time. "Mmm . . . good morning to you too."

She slides her hips over my cock, both of us gasping as her lips rub against me and I feel her clit drag down my shaft. Sarah sits up more, and I get a chance to look at the body of a goddess. I reach down, rubbing my hands over her waist and slapping her ass lightly. "I couldn't wait anymore. Not when you're in my arms, rubbing that perfect ass of yours against me."

She reaches down, running her fingers through my light chest hair, eyes locked with mine, her face serious as her hips freeze. "How did I get so lucky? Ry, I thought I would die as Jacob's prisoner. Thank you for saving me from hell, setting me free."

My voice is thick as I respond. "You're the one who saved me. I never thought past knocking Jacob off his throne and making him pay for what he did to my dad. It was all nebulous, just being 'King of the Streets'. But now, there's more for me. There's a future with you."

Sarah's eyes never waver from mine as she lowers her body down to kiss me before dangling her breasts in my face. I kiss the silky soft skin tenderly, tracing the deep star-shaped scar on her side with my tongue, marking over it with better memories. I kiss to her nipple, sucking it deep into my mouth, teasing her with swirls of my tongue all around her breast. I trace down her curves with my hand, tracing her ass and delighting at her gasp.

I know that Sarah could probably use a few visits to a good head doctor. The hell she went through can't be cured through a 'kidnapping' and a vacation in upstate New York. I've held her safe and given her space when she's woken up from nightmares or gone into reflective funks. But it's here in bed, I think, that lets her heal the most. I give her what she needs, showing her that there's more than just anger and violence in a relationship. "Show me, baby. Show me how good you want to feel."

Sarah smiles and throws her hair back over her shoulder in a dark wave that makes my cock twitch as she lifts herself up. Reaching down, she spreads the lips of her pussy to show me just how wet she is as she positions herself. I watch, my eyes widening as a glistening droplet of her moisture drips from her pussy to fall on the head of my cock, disappearing into the shiny wetness already there.

She lowers herself onto my cock, and I smile as she mewls and arches her hips, taking what she needs. With Sarah, I never tease, never do anything but give her what she wants. Reaching down, I place my thumb over the shiny pearl of her clit as she works to take me in deep, inch by inch.

"Oh, fuck," Sarah gasps. She reaches down with her right hand, and I interweave our fingers, locking her hand against my chest. Sarah stills for a moment, just relishing the feeling of fullness as she adjusts to my size. After a moment, she grinds against me, my steely hard cock surrounded by the heat of her tight pussy all the way to the base. "Fuck, Ry, I need you . . . to move."

As Sarah rides me, I oblige, thrusting up into her as she rolls her hips, holding our thrust for a moment at the point where she's completely full before we do it all over again. Sarah's hips roll to meet me every time, welcoming me in as she squeezes, milking me. She cries out, and I know she's close, so I start moving my thumb to strum her clit in time with our strokes. Her fingers tighten on my chest, scratching the skin, but I don't care, as she cries out again. Her body detonates as shudders rack her from head to toe, the spasms triggering my own orgasm, and I fill her with my seed.

Sarah collapses onto my chest, her head smacking my shoulder, but I barely feel it as I hold her, letting her settle completely on top of me, pulling my free hand out to wrap around her and hold her safe and warm as my cock stays buried inside her and our hearts slow. Sarah breathes heavily into my ear before chuckling dreamily. "I was right. This is definitely a good morning."

I turn my head to peek at her, memorizing her mussed hair, rosy cheeks, and satisfied, amused smile. "And as long as you want it, I'll say good morning with you like this every damn day."

The clock picks that minute to switch on, a local radio show turning on. *"The Hot 102.5! Playing the hits that get your morning going!"*

Sarah grumbles and turns her head, smacking my clock radio. "I wish we didn't have to come back to *that.*"

"I'll talk with my boss," I joke, taking the opportunity to nuzzle and nibble on a delectable ear. "Maybe I can get a pay raise enough to afford one of those newfangled clock radios that'll play MP3s."

Sarah laughs, sighing happily as I lick her earlobe before turning her head back and kissing my lips. "Speaking of the *boss*, isn't your brother supposed to be here soon?"

I grumble. She's right. Still, the feeling of her body pressed against mine is tempting. If it weren't that Marcus has the keys and codes to my penthouse and probably still hasn't broken his habit of just walking in whenever he's expected, I'd be tempted to go another round with Sarah. I mean, until about two weeks ago, this was his home too. Still, to have a whole morning of wanton frolicking with Sarah . . .

She sees the frustration in my eyes and smiles. "Don't worry. Rygirl is still right here for you, and you can have me all you want later. Go grab a shower. I'll go get the coffee going."

I pull her down, kissing her forehead tenderly. "I know Marcus is gonna be here soon, so okay. I need to shower, but still, I just want to stay here with you."

Sarah giggles and climbs off me, giving me the chilling and erotic sight of her scarred back and amazing ass. I've spent hours over the past week kissing each of those scars, but it'll be a long time before I can heal the pain. Still, the look she gives me as she sashays over to the hook on the back of the bedroom door and gets the long, purple silk robe I bought her reassures me. "Go get cleaned up, and I'll start the coffee."

She leaves the bedroom, and I get out of bed, heading to the bathroom with a huge grin on my face. She thinks she's lucky, but I'm one lucky man.

CHAPTER 17

SARAH

*P*adding to the kitchen as I tighten the belt on my robe, I make a beeline for the coffee machine. While Ryker might not be a great cook, he's compensated with the best technology money can buy. And a coffee machine that freshly grinds the beans before making some of the best stuff you'll find outside a coffee house? Perfect. Caffeine, quickly and in mass quantities, coming right up.

I hit the button on the machine, deciding to go with the Honduran blend today. Leaning back against the counter, I look around at the penthouse. I can't believe I'm here, safe and happy. Sure, Ryker's penthouse is luxurious, but that means nothing to me. I don't mean to be ungrateful, but I had that at Jacob's place. Luxury doesn't matter to me. We could be back in that broken-down warehouse that Ryker used as a safe house. As long as I have him, I'm happy.

The coffee machine beeps while Ryker's still in the shower, and I pour myself a steaming cup. Reaching across, I grab the sugar and add in two big spoonfuls, the perfect amount for me, before sipping and sighing deeply as the delicious brew immediately finishes waking me up. Morning sex with Ryker is . . . well, *all* sex with Ryker is fabulous, but I also tend to get worn out and want to go back to sleep because it's so dreamy. But not with this stuff.

The doorbell rings and I set down my cup. I head into the foyer by the elevator, checking the video camera feed, and I see that it's Marcus, along with a woman. I chuckle. No wonder Marcus used the doorbell. I thumb the intercom. "Come on in, guys."

A minute later, the front door opens and Marcus comes in. With him is Kendra, a feisty sparkplug of a woman whom I met the very first night that Ryker kidnapped me from Jacob. At first, I was unsure about her. She seemed to be enmeshed in Ryker's world so well, and she is a beautiful, albeit deadly, woman. With tattoos covering her right arm, brown hair done up in twin braids, and a strong jawline, I thought I'd be put off by her sometimes rough around the edges demeanor. Instead, I've enjoyed the times she and I have been able to talk, limited though it might be. "Someone's got a freshly fucked look on their face."

Marcus looks aghast at Kendra's greeting, but I have to chuckle, smiling. "What can I say? It's damn good coffee," I joke back, raising my mug in a toast. "What do you say, Kendra? Want a little cream with your sugar?"

Kendra laughs and spins around one of the dining table chairs, sitting down and leaning against the low back casually. "No thanks. I like my coffee like way I like my men."

"You mean any way you can get it?" Marcus jokes. It's another thing I like about Marcus's evolution—he's growing more comfortable with showing both sides of his personality. Inside, he's still the thoughtful guy who helped take care of me when Ryker was out taking care of business, but he never would have let Kendra joke with me before, or have joked back with her. Before now, he was Ryker's right-hand man, kicking ass and taking names and holding the line. Now, he's developing into . . . more.

Kendra turns a light shade of pink but doesn't say anything. She's lower in rank within the gang, even if I suspect she's quickly climbing the ranks.

"Hey, you eaten yet?"

"Nope, but I appreciate the coffee," Kendra says, getting up and walking into the kitchen like she owns the place to grab a mug, obviously remembering where they're kept. I remember our first real conversation, where she bluntly told me that she'd never slept with Ryker, had no designs on him whatsoever, and good luck with that. She'd raised a finger with each of her list of items like they were bullet points and then turned her hand to flip me off. I wasn't sure whether to be relieved or offended at the time, but ultimately, it's made it more comfortable for us to be friendly.

Marcus grabs a mug of coffee as well, and we settle into the living room. "How're you doing? Everything okay since you guys got back?"

I can tell he wants to ask so much more, but he's trying to be tactful. It's another of my favorite things about Marcus. He can be sweet, kind, even a bit quiet in private, but I've seen him in action, too. When shit needs to get done, he turns it on and is a dominant badass who demands respect from his crew. It's fun and more than a little entertaining to watch him switch between personas. It reminds me of acting when I'd have to get into character. But for Marcus, it's not fake or acting, just two sides of the same coin. As he develops, I'm curious to see if the two sides blend more or if he keeps them separate, keeping his sweet side hidden in favor of being the new hardass boss in town.

"I'm good. Actually, I'm great. I've got another meeting with the police today."

"You going to talk to the cops?" Kendra interrupts, surprised. "No offense, but I wouldn't go into Police Plaza without being unconscious or dead."

"Relax," I reply, smiling. "Ryker's going with me, and I'm not expecting it to be anything more than a formality. They'll have to leave Jacob's case open, of course, but nobody's talking. Also, this afternoon, a lawyer's going to come by to talk about Jacob's will. I don't really give a shit about anything of his, but I am the listed next of kin. Jacob had no heirs."

Marcus nods in acceptance. "Good, good. Let me know if you need a guy for the money management. I know someone. He's clean and everything, but talented at making your money work for you."

"Thanks. I'm just gonna see what the lawyer says and go from there. I don't even know what all Jacob had other than the house. I mean, you guys blew up his restaurants."

I feel Ryker walk in behind me, his presence filling the space as he offers a handshake-hug combination to Marcus. He sits down, close but not crowding me, letting me always know that I'm safe. "I think it was the best bit of urban renewal this city's done in twenty years. Actually, Marcus, do me a favor. Arrange a car and driver for going down to talk to the cops. I just want to relax today."

Marcus laughs. "Yeah, I can do that. Think of it as a retirement gift."

Ryker shifts to all business. Kendra brings him a cup of coffee, and he takes a sip, giving me a thankful nod. Somehow, he knew. "Okay, so enough with the pleasantries. Let's talk this through. How do you want to handle this?"

Kendra interrupts, her eyes flashing between Ryker and me. "Ryker, no offense, but are you sure about this?

Are you really ready to give up everything you worked for?"

Ryker strokes my hand, reassuring me before he says anything. "Kendra, I did exactly what I always planned on doing, delivering justice to the man who killed my father. Yes, I planned on running this city after that, but plans change. Marcus is the man for that job, and I have other things to consider now."

"Did you make him do all of this?" Kendra asks me in her usual blunt manner. "Some kind of pussy magic?"

"Kendra, I didn't force Ryker. He wanted out of the life, and after what Jacob was like . . . well, let's just say I wish *all* of you were out of the life. But I understand the reality of things. So Ryker and I are making a choice for ourselves."

Kendra looks at Marcus, who gives her a look that makes me wonder. *Nah, couldn't be.* She doesn't seem to see it though. "You know, I back Marcus all the way. Just making sure. And Sarah, you're all right. Probably the closest thing I have to a girlfriend, but don't be calling me for shopping and shit, 'kay? You might be just fine rolling in a silk robe, but I'm a bit more rugged. I don't even have a pair of high heels."

"Thanks, Kendra, and don't knock a silk robe till you've curled up in one. Maybe I'll get you one and then you'll see for yourself. Seriously, though, I appreciate that you've always had Ryker's and Marcus's backs and aren't the least bit scared to call them on their shit. So do me a favor."

"What's that?" Kendra asks. "Frappes and manicures?"

I laugh, shaking my head. "No, I want you to keep checking on Marcus and watching his back."

"Now that's something I can do."

CHAPTER 18

*A*fter breakfast, Marcus and I go down to my basement gym. I've used a lot of crummy, dirty 'dungeons' in my time, but I have to admit that having my own gym in the basement of this building has been a pampering I like.

As I roll out my shoulders, Marcus gets right to the point. "All right, Ryker, I know you said you needed a vacation, and I understood. I didn't call you except for big issues the whole week you were up in Niagara or wherever the hell it was you guys went."

I laugh lightly. We didn't get anywhere near Niagara Falls. Just me, Sarah, and a cabin in the woods over-looking a lake. "Which I appreciate."

"Good, but you know I need you here now, right? We've got to establish our control. It's only been a few weeks since you killed Waters."

I cross the room to the wall of 'accessories' that I like to use and select a set of medium-intensity resistance bands. They're good for warming up, and I want to work my back today. "I know. But this transition needs to happen as rapidly as possible, Marcus. I'm getting out of the life. Sarah is my priority now."

Marcus gives me a questioning look, waiting while I do my shoulder exercises, the whole time looking uncertain even after I just told Kendra the same thing. "You're really doing this, giving up everything for her after working so hard for years? I know you keep saying it, but damn, part of me still doesn't believe it. Or maybe I just don't want to."

I think back over the years, fighting for every scrap until I could make a name for myself, the nightmares after my early jobs when my stomach would roll with what I'd had to do, earning respect bit by bit as I proved myself to the crews on the ground in this city. No one thought I had what it took. I started from there, fighting my way up and making a name for myself. Yes, the last few years have been better, controlling and strategizing from the top of the hierarchy as boss, but it still comes at a price—one I'm no longer willing to pay.

Instead of explaining all of this to Marcus, I go over to the pullup bar, clipping the band to the post between my feet before grabbing the bar overhead, making each pull harder as I go up. I shake out my arms again and reply. "Yep, she's it, the one and only for me. I told you when it all happened that she's more important than anything. Except maybe you, man. And regardless of what Jacob Waters may have been, Sarah's not part of this world."

"I can see that," Marcus says, agreeing.

I start my first set of pull ups, going all the way up and down as I feel my muscles work. After ten, I let go and shake out. "You know better than anyone that I don't do things half-assed, taking care of this city or loving her. I've got to do what I've got to do. The city's yours, Marcus. Don't fail it."

Marcus hears my challenge and smirks, pulling off his shirt and rolling his own shoulders out. "Fail it, huh? Let's see who fails first then. Alternating sets of eight?"

We go to it. Marcus has always been not only my little brother, but my biggest supporter and the person who pushes me to be the best I can be. At least until Sarah. We go back and forth, the rules long established until we both fail at the same point, neither of us getting more than six reps on the last set. Leaning against the wall, Marcus chuckles. "I still say you cheated on that last one."

"I'm a crook. Of course I cheated," I joke back. "So, you feeling better about all of this?"

Marcus laughs, shrugging. "Holy shit, man, gimme a little time to let it sink in still. How you wanna do this then?"

I undo the band and head over to the bent-over row machine, sliding on plates until I'm sure I'm challenged. "Just like we talked about before my vacation. You're gonna run the show, be the face, and I'll be the man behind the curtain. You've been doing street-level lieutenant stuff for a while now, so it's just a slight step up. Let everyone think I'm running it quietly for a while so it's not like it's happening so fast, but it's all you. Your decisions, your rewards. And your consequences."

"That I've got no problem with," Marcus says as I start my first set of heavy rows. "But what about on the big level? All the bosses around town know you're the king now, man. How are you going to get them to accept my word around here?"

"We'll transition," I reply, switching arms on my exercise. "Any meetings, we both go, so they get just as used to you as me. Then, once they all know you, I step back. By then, the word should be out that you're the man in charge. Still, keep me in the loop so I know what's going on, and we'll transition as slowly as you need. You can keep me on as your 'business consultant', because I've always got your back if you need anything, brother. Deal?"

Marcus gestures with his hand, and I get out of the way so he can do his set. "Deal. So first up, the streets. They've been on lock now for two weeks, Ryker. I'm worried that if it goes much longer, the pressure cooker's gonna get too much. Everyone knows our crew's the control valve. I think we're ready to roll back full-steam for the boys and the girls. Junkies are getting pretty fucking antsy, and I had to spot a few girls some cash to cover their bills for their kids."

I sigh, knowing Marcus is right. I wish there were a magic wand I could wave to get rid of the junkies and the street girls, but there isn't. The game's been going on longer than I've been alive. We just have to make sure it's as bloodless as possible. "Yeah, you're right. Let loose on the grip and let things go on like they always have, but make sure the beat cops keep a close watch on the girls because it could get ugly at first. I don't want any of the johns thinking they get some back-to-school special or something. And if we're going to get Kendra working closer with you, I want her out there. Have her check in on the girls. You know they'd rather talk to another woman if they run into issues. Plus, none of the asshole johns are going to fuck with her if there's an issue. Just be ready to back her up if she needs it."

Marcus nods, then laughs lightly. "Kendra doesn't need backup. Everyone's afraid of her."

It's true. Back when she was in high school, just as she was getting into the life, an ill-informed pimp decided to try and 'recruit' Kendra. He ended up in the hospital with his left arm broken in three places and five teeth missing. The story on the street says that she was a breath away from chopping his dick clean off but decided the threat of it was enough . . . that time. Since then, nobody's dared fuck with her that way. "Still, remember, just as I brought you up as my lieutenant, and I'm going to groom you to be king, Kendra needs to be groomed to take your old role. Or at least part of it."

Marcus thinks for a moment, and I can see him mentally going down his bullet-pointed list in his head while I get the next set of my exercise in. "Okay. And the docks. Ships are already coming in back on schedule, so we're good there, business as usual. Airport takeover is a done deal too, although we probably need one more meet-n-greet with Arnie down there so he's settled down comfortably."

"What about the guards at the airport?" I ask as Marcus gets himself into position. "Probably need to pay a few to keep them on our side."

Marcus grins even as he grunts through the exertions of his work. "Already on that. We had a partner team on the take already, and one of them wants a cushy, safe job off the beat because he's got a new wife and baby. I worked out their transfer, and both cops went happily. So no new outgoing funds, and we've got a senior duo placed inside the airport now. Still gotta tap-dance with the Feds, but that's nothing new."

I laugh because he's so fucking brilliant, pulling shit like that like it's nothing when it's genius. "You did all that without my even needing to know about it. You see, Marcus? You've got this easily."

My praise helps him grin even more, and we finish up our workout. As I pull my shirt back on, there's a knock on the door, and Sarah comes in, Kendra right behind her. "Hey, Ryker."

"We'll be up in a minute, babe," I tell Sarah. "Give me and Marcus another minute?"

"Sure. Just wanted to remind you that we'll need to leave in about fifteen minutes to get to Police Plaza on time."

I nod, glancing at Marcus. "Our car?"

"I took care of it," Kendra replies. "You'll have a Towncar outside the building in ten minutes."

The two leave, and I shake my head. "She's gonna be good for you, Marcus."

Marcus shrugs, placing his right hand on my shoulder to get my undivided attention. "Ryker, this isn't about business. Listen, you've always lived balls to the wall, but still, this is some crazy-ass shit. You know I've got your back no matter what, and if that includes taking the keys to the castle so you can settle with some pussy, I just have one thing to say."

I growl at his calling Sarah 'some pussy', but before I can lay into him, he gives me a grin. It was his way of pointing it out. *Message received, Marcus.* I know some asshole in the future could use her as a weakness, but that's why I want out of the game. "Point being, you're a damn lucky bastard that Sarah-fucking-Desjardins would give a low-class fucker like you the time of day, much less fall in love with you like some twisted-up TV fairy tale. Don't fuck it up, Ryker. She ain't a princess. She's a damn queen. And you'd best not forget it."

I reach out, hugging my brother and clapping him across his sweaty back. "I haven't stopped thinking the same thing, and I'm never gonna forget it either. Thanks for understanding. Now, go get your ass a shower down here while I go upstairs and do the same. I still gotta pick out a suit to wear for going to Police Plaza."

"If you want my advice, Crown Royal purple with leather trim is always good," Marcus says with a smirk. "And if you can, one of those bigass hats with a two-foot-long feather and a cane."

"I think I'll take Sarah's advice instead. Business suit," I reply, making Marcus roll his eyes. "What?"

"I see how it is. Find the love of your life and suddenly, your brother's advice is no good any more. Next thing you know, she's gonna make you dress and act decently and shit."

Heading for the door, I laugh. "You never know, man. I might just learn what the hell a napkin is for. Besides, she might be good for you too."

"What for?" Marcus asks.

I turn back, grinning. "You curse too damn much."

CHAPTER 19

SARAH

*W*alking into Police Plaza seems like it'd be the scariest thing anyone could have to do on most days. In addition to the normal assortment of people under arrest who would rather be *anywhere* but Police Plaza, the officers are stoically hostile and I can feel their eyes roving up and down my body, judging me and questioning why I'm there with Ryker.

I know they're all condemning me in their heads. Wife —well, now officially the widow—of the town's biggest crime boss, now seen with the man who's moving into his spot. It's got to be raising some eyebrows, and if it weren't that Ryker commands a lot of fear, I'm sure some of the tabloid scum around *The Post* would already be saying something.

Some of the officers we pass as we cross the 'bullpen' were loyal to Jacob, and with his murder, they probably suspect more than they can prove. I don't care. I recognize one of the detectives on duty behind his desk. Back when he was a beat cop, he'd brought me home to Jacob even after I told him about the abuse. I think about saying something to Ryker about it but decide not to. It would just cause trouble that we don't need.

I'm ushered into a Deputy Chief's office and the secretary offers me a coffee, politely dipping her chin at my murmured refusal before leaving. In the silence, I glance over at Ryker. "Any reason you chose the blue suit?" I ask as he brushes a bit of dust off his pant leg. "Considering where we are?"

Ryker gives me an amused smirk. "Wanted to coordinate with the lingerie you're wearing."

I laugh, feeling a tremble of desire. It's strange how just a slight change makes all the difference. If Jacob had said something like that, I'd have been shaking in fear. But with a slight change in tone and the look in his eyes, Ryker makes me feel like the most desired woman in the world. "Ryker—"

"Shh," Ryker says, shaking his head as he points out the window. "What they know, and what they can prove, remember?"

It's one of the lessons he's taught me, although I already saw it in action with Jacob. The cops can *know* everything Ryker's up to, and what I'm up to, but it doesn't matter. The important thing is to make sure they can't *prove* anything if they wanted to. And this office is most likely bugged.

A moment later, Deputy Chief Warren Matthews comes in, puffed up considerably in his dress uniform. His having us wait was probably part of his power play. "Hello, Mrs. Waters. Thank you for coming down."

"Of course, Chief Matthews. But I've decided to go by my maiden name for now, so Desjardins, if you don't mind."

He hears the commanding tone to my voice and inclines his head thoughtfully, his eyes slowly moving toward Ryker. He seems to make an evaluation of the situation, although I'm sure he already had an idea of what's going on. "I wanted to say how sorry I am for your loss, Mrs. . . . . Sarah," he says. If he can't use my last name, he'll just cast his disrespect by using my first name only, I suppose. "Your husband was a very well-respected man in our city. He had many friends within our department and always supported us very well come fundraising time."

I can feel the smarmy slickness as he speaks about Jacob like he was some honorable man who helped folks out of the goodness of his heart. I'm just about to give him a piece of my mind, sharing just what an abusive asshole Jacob really was, when Ryker places his hand over mine. *Don't,* his eyes tell me calmly. *Remember, he knows.*

Ryker's right. The Chief does know. All of the bullshit

that he's talking right now is for show. Matthews most likely got his position within the department by kissing the right asses. We live in that sort of town. And one of the asses he had to kiss the most was certainly Jacob Waters's. So for Matthews, he's worried about losing out on the gravy train. As if the six-figure salary he's probably getting isn't enough of a gravy train, considering how ineffective he is.

Instead of replying, I give Ryker a small nod of thanks. He gives my fingers a slight squeeze and looks at the Chief. "Chief Matthews, this is a difficult time, as I'm sure you're aware. What, exactly, is it that you need from Miss Desjardins today?"

"I'm sorry, and you are?" the Chief retorts, as if everyone in the building didn't know exactly who was walking in the front door as soon as we stepped out of the Towncar. It's still there, parked blatantly in a 'police only' zone, with two of Ryker's men standing guard, looking for all the world like Secret Service men. The innocent residents of the city must think the Vice President's in town or something.

Instead of being rattled or offended, Ryker offers his hand in what appears to be a crushing handshake by the wince in Matthews's face. "We already know each other very well, *Captain* Matthews, but perhaps you need a reminder. I'm Ryker Johns. We've met on numerous occasions, some good, some perhaps . . . less so."

Matthews turns slightly red at the use of the title, 'Captain', and I remind myself to ask Ryker what the connection is. "Yes, indeed, we have. It's been a few years. You look different now."

"As do you," Ryker replies. "Last time I saw you, you were wearing an off-the-rack suit that screamed 'cop' while looking very . . . uncomfortable in a back alley. The Deputy Chief's uniform looks good on you. I definitely approved."

The implied threat is clear, even in a simple use of the past tense, and I have to smirk. Ryker's playing this man like a guitar, and the Chief is clearly in over his head. "Well, then, are you a friend of Mrs. Waters now?"

He's returned to calling me by my married name. I'm not sure if it's intentional or by accident, but the tension is damn near stifling as the men eye each other. Ryker replies with a sarcastic tilt to his voice. "Yes, Miss Desjardins and I are . . . friends. I'm supporting her in this difficult time. In a town like this, finding friends who will respect you is sometimes the difference between life and death."

Matthews looks like he's about to shit himself, either in anger at being threatened or in fear—I'm not sure which—as he turns to me. "You know, Mrs. Waters, if I may be so bold, I'd consider carefully the company you keep in this town. Your husband had quite the reputation, and with him barely in the grave, there are certain expectations for a widow."

"Excuse me?" I ask, coldly furious. How dare this asshole tell me to consider my abusive prisoner of a husband now that I'm finally free of his controlling terror. I inhale deeply, preparing to lay into him, when I realize it's a ploy. I can see the greedy excitement in his eyes. He's trying to needle me to say something I shouldn't, and I need to shut this down.

I let out my breath and put on a smile that's been dredged from the darkest portions of my brain, the areas that still remember what my 'husband' did to me. It's a predator's smile, and right now, I feel like Jaws himself would be scared of me. "Chief, I know better than anyone what my husband was. It's my understanding that the investigation into his death is currently underway but you don't really have any leads. If that's right, am I needed for anything else? I have another appointment today, if that's all this was about."

Matthews flounders under my smile for a moment, visibly shaken that I didn't lose my temper. Obviously, he thought he'd done enough to provoke me into saying something stupid. He was nearly right, but luckily, I realized before I stumbled into his trap. Ryker's saying anything probably would've just set off more alarms. Still, the look he gives me as Matthews's lip curls warms me even more inside.

"Well, no," Matthews says. "Unfortunately, while our investigation is still in the beginning stages, there isn't a lot that we can do. *Associates* of your late husband seem to have mistakenly cleaned most of the crime scene before our people were called in. Other than being able to say that your husband and the woman—"

"Constanza," I interrupt. "Her name was Constanza, and she was the housekeeper."

Matthews swallows. "Yes, of course. Other than being able to tell that they were killed with different bladed weapons, our forensics team has very little to go on. I'm not going to lie, Mrs. . . . sorry, Miss Desjardins, but I doubt we'll ever be able to get justice for Jacob Waters. Still, we have detectives working on the case."

"I'm sure you do," Ryker says. "Are Detectives Schroeder and Lamonica on the taskforce?"

Matthews does his best to repress a growl, but he nods. "Yes, they're two of our most senior homicide detectives."

"I see. Well, I hope they can find the time for a thorough investigation after their lunchtime visit to The Fruit Stand is over."

Matthews looks like he's about to explode, but he says nothing. "Thank you for coming in. If any new evidence arises, we'll notify you."

I stand up, ready to leave. "Don't lose a wink of sleep over my husband, sir. His justice was served." The chief's eyebrows raise, and I can tell he's trying to decipher my statement. Before he can decide, I stand and offer my hand. "I trust that we won't see each other again. Thank you."

He nods his chin once. "Of course, Miss Desjardins. Please let me know if you need anything. Our department will help in any way we can for Mr. Waters's widow."

I don't bother responding and simply walk out, Ryker following quietly behind me, although I can feel eyes watching us. Outside, his two men are still standing with the car, although with a wave of his hand, one of them turns and walks away. He'll catch the subway back home.

Inside the car, I can't take the stress anymore. I'm done for right now. I don't care about the connection Ryker and Matthews have or what Ryker knows about the homicide detectives. Any of it. I collapse against Ryker's chest as his arms pull me close. "Well, that was a huge waste of fucking time."

"Yeah, but at least we got an idea where they're at. Right now, the cops are still adjusting. For an old guard like Matthews, he's scared and trying to figure out if we'll play ball with him or if he needs to try and mount some sort of Quixotic crusade and come after us. That or just retire. After the dust settles, Marcus and I might need to do a little PR with the boys in blue and give them some reassurances."

I sigh, and he rubs his hand over my hair, petting me, but somehow, it's calming. Glancing up front, I see that the driver's put up the privacy screen, so I wiggle closer and Ryker pulls me into his lap, his attentions turning more heated. He cups my face in his hands, stroking my cheeks with his thumbs as he looks into my eyes. "Listen to me. You did nothing wrong and Jacob got exactly what he deserved. And now, you will get the life you deserve if it's the last thing I do."

I smile, knowing he's right and that I'm exactly where I should be—in his arms. "I have the life I want right this moment."

Ryker smiles and covers my mouth with sweet, teasing kisses that both lighten my dark mood and turn the small ember of heat that I felt the entire interview, watching his powerful handling of the chief, into a roaring inferno. His tongue teases along the seam of my lips, lightly demanding entrance, and I obey, opening and entwining my tongue with his. He nibbles my bottom lip as his hand lifts to cup my breast, tantalizing the stiffening peak as I moan and press my breast higher for him.

This is so different from Jacob. Now, I *want* to be with him in the back of a car, tugging my skirt up to give him access to my body. I *want* to feel his hands on my skin, the feel of his tongue in the valley between my breasts, licking electric tingles across my body as I clutch at him.

Ryker moves to unbutton my top, and I turn to straddle him, my skirt pooling around my waist to let my legs rest outside his hips. I push my fingers into his hair, pulling him between my breasts, and wordlessly, he gives me what I want as he kisses along the top curve. He slides my top off, giving him more access to me, leaving me in just my bra. Instead of the falsely sexy Agent Provocateur lingerie Jacob forced me to wear, Ryker took me shopping on vacation, and I'm wearing one of those bras, a solid, slightly old-fashioned black cotton t-shirt bra that feels amazing. Ryker nibbles on my skin, his lips following each nip of his teeth to set my pulse racing even faster.

Pulling the left cup of my bra down, he groans at the sight of my hard nipple and dives in like a starving man, sucking and licking and making me mad for him. I feel him hard and throbbing between my legs, but patience is a virtue. "Mmm, that's so good, baby. Make me feel . . . oh, God, Ryker."

Repeating the movements on the other breast, I can't help myself as I grind along the hard ridge of his cock through his pants. Ryker pulls back, reaching under my skirt to squeeze my ass cheeks and kiss up my neck to look into my eyes. "That's it, honey. Rub that sweet little pussy on my fat cock. Arch your back for me, give me these pretty pink nipples, and grind your clit on me. That's it, just like that."

Just hearing him talk to me like that turns me on even more, and with a cry, I shatter. Shaking, I whimper as my orgasm ripples through me, Ryker pulling me tightly to him. He presses my body to his as he thrusts his cock against me, prolonging my orgasm even separated by layers of fabric. I'm boneless, suddenly exhausted from all the drama and tension, and of course, the amazing orgasm I just had in the back of a moving car. Ryker holds me, returning to running his hands through my hair.

It's minutes later before I feel time start up again and the hum of traffic outside the darkened windows. It doesn't matter. Ryker holds me secure as he helps me fix my bra and top. When I'm more or less put together again, he strokes my cheek with the back of his hand, looking deep into my eyes. "We've got this, Sarah. Everything's gonna be fine. Okay?"

I smile, cupping his cheek. "As long as you're with me, I know I'll be safe."

CHAPTER 20

After the tense morning meeting, I tried to get Sarah to reschedule the appointment with the lawyer, but she wasn't having it, saying she'd rather get everything done in one fell swoop and deal with the fallout later. Riding the elevator up to the penthouse, I can hardly believe that this is the same scared, shaken woman I met just a few weeks ago.

Sure, she's still got issues from Jacob, some of which she may never fully recover from. But right now, watching her as she gives me a shy little smile across the empty elevator, all I can think is, that's my girl, strong and resilient, even more so than she realizes.

"What're you thinking about?"

I chuckle, leaning against the side of the elevator. "That you played the Chief like a fiddle. And afterward . . ."

"Yeah well, if this elevator were any slower, I'd see if we

could get a repeat performance in here," Sarah teases. "I know you want to see me in my old schoolgirl skirt from the show."

"And just how would you know about that?"

Sarah laughs. "You sometimes talk in your sleep, especially if someone is talking back. One night, I woke up from a nightmare, and you were talking in your sleep. I didn't wake you. I just started talking and you mumbled back."

I feel heat creep up my neck. "What else did I say?"

Sarah gives me a mysterious smile, biting her lip. "Nothing bad or I'd have said something."

We get to the penthouse, and my cock is raging in my pants, but now isn't the time. We've only got twenty minutes until the lawyer gets here, and neither of us has had anything to eat since a light breakfast. Thankfully, there's a note on the fridge.

You tell anyone about this, and I get mad- K.

"Tell anyone about what?" I ask, opening the fridge and seeing two plates of sandwiches, complete with pickles.

"Did she get this from a deli or something?" Sarah asks as I take out the plates. "They look delish."

"Nope, no deli is around this building. And these are our plates," I note, unwrapping the plastic from my plate. "BATC. Bacon, avocado, turkey and cheese. My favorite."

"This one's a club," Sarah notes. Picking up the pickle, she crunches in, nodding her approval.

"Okay, no matter what, I'm taking that girl shopping. She doesn't have to get heels or a dress. I don't care. Maybe I'll even take her to a salon."

I chuckle. That'll be the day. "Okay. Just don't be surprised if she causes a scene."

"We both might," Sarah jokes. We tear into our lunches, eating as we lean over the counter to keep the dining room table clean. Knowing there will likely be paperwork to go over, we want that space clear and open. There's a buzz from the lobby just as we finish up, and I go over, checking the video intercom.

"Hello?"

The man who's waiting looks the part of a lawyer, and not a legal eagle type either. With round-rimmed glasses, a receding hairline, and a gray suit, he looks just like Marcus told me when we investigated him. Patrick Green is your normal run-of-the-mill lawyer. "Mr. Johns? My name's Patrick Green. I have an appointment."

"Come on up," I say, reaching into the closet next to the alcove and quickly opening the gun safe I have in there. It's keyed to my fingerprint, and I normally always carry the Beretta, except this morning, with going to Police Plaza and all.

When the elevator dings, the pistol's inside my coat in

a belt holster, but Green's alone, looking slightly nervous as he steps out. His briefcase is far too skinny to have a gun in it, and the way he's walking, I don't think he's a threat. Still, it doesn't hurt to be safe, and I don't let my guard down until he's sitting at the table. He opens his case, revealing a thin file folder and an iPad. Sarah comes out of the bathroom, where she was brushing her teeth quickly, giving him a smile. "Mr. Green?"

"Mrs. . . . sorry, I forgot. You wish to be called Miss Desjardins," Green says, blushing slightly. I remain standing, watching them quietly from the kitchen counter where I can see everything Green's doing, even under the table. "I'm glad you agreed to meet with me. The sooner I can get your signatures on some paper-work, the faster we can get Jacob Waters's estate through the probate courts."

I lean back, not relaxing but looking that way as Green opens his file folder. Sarah seems sure there won't be any problems because she just doesn't care about Jacob's money. But I wouldn't put it past that jerk to have done some crazy shit in his will just to fuck her over from the grave. And after Chief Matthews's obvious fandom of Jacob, I'm reserving judgment on this guy for now.

Green reaches into his coat, but he's out a moment later with a pair of gel ball pens. "All right, Miss Desjardins—"

Sarah smiles, shaking her head. "Please, call me Sarah. Thanks for the respect, but I'd rather keep this casual."

"Of course . . . Sarah," Green says with a hesitant smile. He glances at me, and I can see he knows my reputation but is professional enough to not let it get to him too much. "Well, Jacob Waters's estate is rather straightforward considering the size. Is there anything specific you're concerned about before we begin going line-by-line?"

Sarah leans forward, taking the papers and looking through them quickly. "Uh, no. Mr. Green, I honestly don't know anything about Jacob's money. He didn't discuss finances with me at all, so I'm not sure what to expect."

Green raises an eyebrow, but his voice doesn't shake at all. "Well, that does change things a bit. Stop me if you have any questions as we work through the accounts because there are quite a few."

Sarah looks a little overwhelmed and gives me a little glance. "Okay. I guess I didn't realize it was going to be that complicated."

Green looks at Sarah, obviously appraising her, looking for something. I watch him carefully too, noting that he's not studying Sarah like so many other people have. After a moment, he seems to see what he wants and smiles genuinely. "Of course. That's what I'm here for. If I may say, I didn't know your husband well. I came to be of service to him when my daughter got into some trouble a few years ago. I'll admit, Mr. Waters agreed to write off some debts she had in return for my work on his estate. He always seemed rather . . . intimidating and hard, if I may say so."

He looks at Sarah questioningly, obviously assessing whether his opinion has offended her. I can easily see what he's asking for, and if it were me, I'd be more than happy to grant it. But it's Sarah's call.

I shouldn't have worried. "Look, Mr. Green, Jacob was a cruel and forbidding man," Sarah says, shivering slightly. "He wasn't even a man. He was a monster. I'm just as glad to be out from under his thumb as you obviously are now. I'm guessing you'd like to be done with this whole mess, so walk me through it and then you can consider yourself free of any debt your daughter might have owed to Jacob."

A look of relief washes over Green's face at Sarah's words. He nods, the corners of his mouth tilting up in a faint smile as he turns on his iPad.

Green copies over the files to a flash drive so she can have a digital copy, and the two of them begin going through Jacob Waters's will, taking the time to reference the dozens of bank statements, business reports, real estate holdings, safe deposit box inventory lists, and other documents that detailed Jacob Waters's legal financial life. It's overwhelming, but Sarah listens to it all attentively. "I can't believe I'm gonna have to figure out what to do with all of Jacob's blood money."

"That's just a drop in the bucket," I admit, speaking up. "No offense to Mr. Green, but there's a lot more that Jacob never had in his name. There's at least twice that much out there that's not on any account book that'll see the light of day."

Sarah swallows, and I know I'll have to outline to her more about what I know, but this isn't the time. Instead, she turns her attention back to Mr. Green and Jacob's will. The final tally is staggering, over fifty million dollars to allocate, manage, and assign. There's a silence in the room as everyone processes, and Sarah stills as Mr. Green eyes her. "Miss Desjardins, I'm not an investment banker, but with this amount of money, you could live very comfortably off even the interest of a simple savings account. That may not matter much to you right now, but for all intents and purposes, you are free. Totally free."

Sarah looks up, smiling that soft smile that I've come to recognize as Sarah's thoughtful smile. "Mr. Green, you can say no, but you seem well-versed in this estate. I wonder if you might consider allowing me to hire you to work with my money manager to get this coordinated? Your standard attorney rate would apply. And any debt your daughter may have owed Jacob and any coercion he may have used to get you to work for him is done, as far as I'm concerned."

Green gulps at the gift that's been dropped into his lap, both in letting go of the debt and the potential continued work with the estate. His eyes move slowly from Sarah to me and back again. I can tell that he's a man of conscience, and the idea of working with someone still involved in criminal activity worries him. "That is a kind offer, but I have to admit—"

I raise a hand, getting his attention. "Mr. Green, your work for Sarah would be totally above-board and legal."

He gives me a grateful nod and turns back to Sarah. "Then I'd be happy to stay on to help you sort through and get everything situated the way you'd like. Do you have any ideas on what you'd like to do with the money?"

She sits back for a moment, her gaze dropping to her lap as her brain obviously whirls. She looks at me, and I come over, sitting down and taking her hand. "Sarah, it's yours. Every bloody red cent. You decide what you want to do, what you need to do, and I'll support that. No pressure or opinion here."

She smiles, making her decision as she turns back to Green, nodding. "I do have an idea. I want to start a charity to help victims of domestic violence. Talk with your friend, of course, and invest it so that there's a nest egg, I suppose, just in case. But I want to explore a lot of options. Maybe a shelter, with medical treatment and occupational training for the women, legal help for restraining orders and divorces, and therapists to help them deal with what they've been through. Whatever they need to get out, get safe, and start fresh."

Mr. Green stares slack-jawed at her, and when he finally speaks again, his voice is thick with emotion. "That sounds rather . . . altruistic. I happen to specialize in tax law, so I'd be delighted to help make that a reality. "

I lean back, pretending I've got something in my eye to hide the feelings that I've got right now. I'm so proud of her that I wish I could fucking give her a round of applause. She's amazing. In a situation where nobody would fault her for taking Jacob Waters's money and running away to the farthest corner of the world to relax away the rest of her life on a beach, she turns it all down. Yeah, she knows that I've got money and I'll take care of her, but she has no idea how much I have. I certainly have nowhere near what Jacob had. But she just puts her faith in me and in our future as she attempts to help women who suffered through what she did. No wonder I love her.

With a few signatures and a promise of future appoints to set up the charity and handle the financials with the money guy Marcus knows, we're soon alone. Sarah goes over to the sofa, collapsing on it as I sit at the other end, picking up her foot and massaging it. She lifts her head, her eyes filled with concern. "What do you think? Am I crazy?"

I keep rubbing her feet, shaking my head. "What I just watched is another reason I love you. Most people would hear cash registers ringing—cha-ching, cha-ching—when someone says they have that kind of money coming their way. I admire what you're doing. Your foundation, charity, whatever you want to call it, I have a feeling it's going to do a lot of good around here."

Sarah sits up, entwining her fingers with mine as she turns around to lean against me, resting her head on my chest. "I love you. More than you know. I would go through that hell with Jacob a thousand times over if it got me here with you like this."

CHAPTER 21

SARAH

*I*t feels a little strange as I look around the hotel ballroom, visually measuring the space for tables, a dance floor, and a stage. It's been a long time since I've done anything public as myself. When Jacob was alive, it was always all about him. I was arm candy and never had the opportunity to speak to the public. Now, I'm planning on a big coming-out party for the Broken Angel Foundation, the name that I decided on with a little help from Kendra, of all people. Too bad she isn't the kind for this sort of event.

Still, I need to go public with all the pain I went through, and the Foundation is the best way to do it. With a smile, I decide this room is just perfect, and I give a nod to Nikolas, the best event planner in the city. "Nikolas, this is it. This is where the Foundation starts."

Nikolas, a great roly-poly bear of a man who's put on parties for everyone from Katy Perry to the Queen of

Norway, nods excitedly. "Agreed. We'll get the date reserved and begin booking the vendors for a rush gig."

I chuckle at Nikolas's thinking of it as a rush gig. I get it, he normally works with timelines of 'this time next year,' but the past two months have been nearly excruciating to me. With most of Jacob's estate tied up in probate court as the governmental cronies who are still smarting over his death drag their heels, I've felt like the past month's been a decade long. Thankfully, not all of Jacob's assets are off-limits to me, and Ryker's been more than helpful. "Nikolas, I'm sure if anyone can get it done, it's you."

He puffs out his chest, threatening to burst the buttons on his shirt, smiling. "Planning a gala in three months' time is crazy, to be quite frank, but yes, if anyone can do it, I can. Now are you sure about getting a crowd?"

I nod, smiling. "You know, I was worried at first, but it's that time of year in Hollywood where there's no awards shows on the calendar but everyone wants to keep themselves on the front page. And surprisingly, more than a few of my old Hollywood associates are willing to make an appearance."

Nikolas grins. "Then first things first. Invitations will go out within a week so we can get on everyone's social calendar. Can you get me a list of guests you're inviting by then?"

"I'll have it sent over by the end of the day," I reply, grinning.

Nikolas nods before basically twirling away from me, phone already to his ear, listing out orders as he walks out to set the date with the hotel representative. It's funny to watch a man who's about as wide as he is tall move so gracefully, almost waltzing around the space as his creative mind already imagines things that will exist here in three months.

With a smile, I head outside, the excitement of making the foundation a reality buzzing around me in a happy cloud. There's still a ways to go. I barely have access to a million of Jacob's money, but it's a start.

"I wish Ryker were here," I murmur to myself as I give the grand ballroom a final look before going out into the lobby. He wanted to come, but today is about the Foundation, and I wanted to test my strength. Since Jacob's death, I've had Ryker, Marcus, or Kendra everywhere I've gone. I want to make sure that, before I put myself forward as a survivor, I've actually survived. So I insisted on coming down here by myself, taking a taxi from the penthouse.

As I cross the lobby, I think about all that I still have to do. Mr. Green set up a meeting with the local archdiocese, and they've got a property that he says can be turned into the shelter site. "It's a good deal," he told me yesterday. "The archbishop gets to do more charity work, and they also get to partially offload a building that they couldn't do anything with."

I understand that part, at least. Most of the big Hollywood movies nowadays are collaborations between studios, everyone pitching in to be able to claim part of the glory or to defray the costs of a bomb. I'm hoping the meeting goes well and we can get the construction crews in the building to take care of renovations within the next few weeks. Winter is coming, sooner than the weather would lead me to believe, and I want the shelter open before the holidays, if possible.

Leaving the hotel, I'm walking around the corner, lost in my mental checklist of what I still have to accomplish over the next few days to make sure this charity ball gets off on the right foot, when I feel a cold hand on my shoulder. I spin around to see a broad-shouldered man who's nearly bursting out of his suit. In his mid-fifties, he's got the almost visible aura of dangerousness that I've come to detect in too many people in my life. He's eye to eye with me, but considering that I'm over six feet in the heels I'm wearing today, he's not short at all. He's crowding into me, sneering as he stares at me with a familiar distaste that I'd hoped I'd never see again.

Stepping back, I quickly put a name to his face. "Viktor, what are you doing here? I haven't seen you since Sal Francisco's funeral."

Viktor—I don't know his last name—is one of those men who could scare me nearly as much as Jacob could. He's just the kind of man who doesn't see other people as human beings but as animals to be consumed. With a grumble, he steps closer to me again. "Shut up with that, bitch. You can't do this, you know."

"Do what?" I ask, trying to keep my voice strong but knowing it's coming out in a terrified little squeak.

Viktor's sneer grows, and he reaches inside his suit coat. I'm worried he's got a gun in there, but after a moment, he pulls his hand out, a business card in his hand that he tucks into the belt of my dress. "Jacob ran this city with an iron fist. The last thing we're gonna let happen is some bitch plaything fuck everything up. He didn't build his organization so you can go play Debbi Do-Right. He's dead, and as I'm the one he was grooming to take over if something happened to him, that makes me the new boss of this city. Not that punk-ass street rat you're shacking up with right now. Me."

The ice in Viktor's unhinged eyes chills me. I tear my eyes away to look around, realizing that we're alone on the street and he's cornered me in an alcove. I'd taken a wrong turn, not sticking to the main streets but turning down a side street.

Looking back at him, I feel my heart begin to tremble again, and my brain starts to darken with the demons that I normally only have to face at night. Still, I remember Ryker and draw strength from his image. "Look, Viktor, I don't really know anything about Jacob or your work with him. You want to try and take over his organization? You're welcome to it. I'm just glad I'm free from him and that I'm with Ryker now."

As soon as I say the name 'Ryker', I know I've made a mistake. Viktor's face turns red and a little vein pops out above his eye. His hand is too fast to even detect as he grabs my throat, not full-out choking me but pushing me against the side of the building we're next to, putting pressure that scares me as he slowly lifts me. My air's being forced from my lungs, the blood pressure building in my brain as he presses upward until my toes are barely touching the ground.

Viktor's hissing like a cat, ranting in his scratchy voice so much that I can only catch a few words over the pulse pounding in my ears. Black flowers begin to bloom in my vision as he tries to lift me higher, my hands doing nothing as they pull down on his arms in a panic. "Little fucker . . . who does he think he is . . . get what's coming . . . won't even see it . . . mine . . . fucking city is mine."

In a desperate move, I stop trying to grab his wrist and weakly claw at his face, regretting that I'd cut my fingernails short. Still, something catches Viktor's attention and he snaps back to me. He lets up, dropping me to hack and cough. I want to go to my knees, but I try to be strong even as I lean against the building for support. He leans in close, growling.

"You tell that little fucker that this town, it's mine. His collection of street hoodlums can't handle what I'm gonna bring against him. If I have any problems out of him, maybe I'll take a play from his book and take his woman."

He grinds his hips against me, and I recoil in disgust, wiggling to try to get away. I'd love to punch him in the balls, but I'm racked by another cough and my legs feel like they're going to collapse. Still, I work up the nerve to speak.

"He's stronger than you. He won't be frightened by you or by anyone you think you have on your side. He's the king now, and there's only one future for you. Either you run, or you're going to end up in an unmarked grave."

Viktor chuckles, stepping back and adjusting the buttons on his suit coat. "Let him try. Oh, and Sarah, one more thing." I look up at him, just like he knew I would, and it happens so fast that I don't see the back-handed slap coming. I just feel the pain explode in my cheek and across my face as I see stars and the black-ness takes me.

CHAPTER 22

"**W**HAT THE FUCK HAPPENED?" I thunder, looking around the room. I'm back at the warehouse that we used as a staging area and safe house for the last fight with Jacob Waters's men. My penthouse isn't the place for this sort of conversation. "Someone needs to talk. Now."

I can't believe this shit. I thought the war was over. Cut the head off the snake and the snake dies. But Jacob's fucking lackey, Viktor Carmichael, who more or less laid low and tried to not get his ass blown away during the conflict, thinks he's somehow in charge now.

I turn his business card over in my fingers, thinking. The fucker had the audacity to give Sarah one of his cards? I re-read it for the fiftieth time since Marcus handed it to me. *Viktor Carmichael. Corporate Consultant for Hire.*

It might as well say *I want to be the king*. But that's not how it works in this town. Men, real men, go out and take what they want by standing up and saying it face to face. They grab their destiny by the throat. Speaking of that, I look over at Sarah, who's shivering as she holds the ice pack over her eye. I know that underneath, she's got a black eye and a small cut where a ring on his finger cut open her cheek when he backhanded her. It's not deep and it shouldn't scar, which is a small favor. She has enough scars as it is. The bloodshot eyes and handprint around her throat will heal too, but it's not the physical marks I'm worried about.

The scariest part is what could've happened if Viktor had gotten more carried away when he was choking her. I could've lost her, and it hits me again that I don't want this for her. She deserves better than to be treated like this, and I thought she would never have to endure something like this again. When I saw her, I was filled with rage unlike anything I've ever known . . . even when Pop died. Sarah's being hurt was like throwing gasoline on an already raging fire.

Marcus, who is nearly as pissed as I am, also looks chagrined. "It's my fault, Ryker. We should've just kept our distance, not flat out let her go alone. When you told me she wanted to take care of the arrangements at the hotel by herself, I thought she was safe. Obviously, that was a mistake."

I shake my head. Marcus doesn't need to take the blame for this. "It's not your fault. If there's anyone to blame for this, it's me. We need to move forward, Marcus."

He nods while giving Sarah an apologetic look. "Full 24/7 guard from here on out for Sarah. That's no problem. Big issue is, we can't let this go unanswered, Ryker. You know that."

My lips curl up in a cold, evil smile as I squat next to Sarah and look into her angry, ashamed but scared eyes. I feel like the world's biggest asshole for breaking my promise to keep her safe, but I have her back and will do whatever's necessary to make sure she never doubts her safety again. I answer Marcus, but my eyes never leave Sarah's.

"Unanswered? Oh, no, this damn sure won't go unanswered. I'll burn this city to the ground and put Carmichael's head on a pike before I let anything happen to Sarah again. He'll pay the ultimate price for daring to hurt her. Never mind his claim that this town is his like he's some bloodlined heir who doesn't have to fucking work for it."

Marcus looks at me worriedly, squatting down next to me and using a quiet voice that only Sarah and I can hear. "Ryker, I know what you want. I want the same thing. But . . . Sarah, I'm not trying to say you don't deserve retribution, but you're both supposed to be getting out of the game. This isn't the sort of thing that lets you walk away."

"What are you saying?" I ask, not looking away from

Sarah. Her lips quiver, and I know that tonight's going to be one of the bad ones, full of nightmares if she even can get to sleep. For every hour of missed sleep, for every nightmare he's given her, I'm going to feel another pint of Viktor's blood on my hands.

"I'm saying we've got to be smart," Marcus says, putting a comforting hand on my shoulder. "We can't just go blowing up the city. He's one man, not even as strong as Jacob was. That line about him bringing forces against us is total bullshit. It's gotta be. We've got this." He emphasizes the last words and sounds certain, and it helps me to settle. He's right, of course. We have to be smart and act with our heads, not our hearts. It was one of the first lessons I taught him when I took over the gang. I know better than to act rashly. I just lost my head for a minute.

I inhale, closing my eyes and letting my mind focus before exhaling slowly, opening my eyes to see Sarah looking at me with love and what I swear is pride. Marcus looks at me, checking to see if I'm ready. Seeing what he needs, he eyes Kendra. "Okay, you're up, Kendra. Tell us what you found out."

Kendra, who's been a flurry of activity over the past few hours and looks it, sips her coffee. "You guys know, Viktor's always been a sick fuck. He started off as Jacob's enforcer down in the Narrows, mostly in charge of intimidation with a side of beating the shit out of anyone who looked at him sideways. But he quickly worked his way up and into Jacob's inner circle. He wasn't Jacob's right-hand man, more his enforcer when he wanted it to be ugly."

"Why wasn't he taken out in the last tussles with Jacob's men?" Marcus asks. "I know he'd have been on the watch list."

"He was out of town, talking with the Russians who control Boston," Kendra says. "Apparently, they happen to like dealing with his particular brand of insanity."

"I'll say," I mutter. "Viktor's a rabid dog."

Kendra hums in agreement. "He's unstable and unpredictable, but his extremeness appeals to the other sick fucks left in Jacob's hierarchy. There aren't a lot of them—no way do they have a numbers advantage—but they're just as unpredictable as he is. Right now, we've confirmed three of them. Viktor's in charge, and he keeps Sam Ryan as his right-hand with Dezzie Alvorado as the outreach man."

"Dezzie?" Marcus asks, surprised. "He flipped on Jacob early once things got hot."

"Yep," I reply with a shake of my head. "He's always been a worm, doing whatever is needed to kiss ass. There's a reason his nickname's *Concha* down in Little Bayamon."

Kendra chuckles while Sarah gives me a questioning look. Before I can explain, Kendra leans over and whispers in Sarah's ear. "It means he's a pussy." For the first time since I came into the warehouse, she cracks a smile, even if it's a pained one.

I turn to Kendra. "I'm going after them. All of them. I want to send a final, unequivocal message that anyone who's thinking of messing with me or Sarah will understand. Where can I find them?"

"Viktor used to be seen in the Narrows near a deli, but according to our people, he's not there anymore. Dezzie and Sam are still at their old haunts."

I nod, thinking. I don't want this to be the same type of destruction that I unleashed when I went after Jacob Waters. The city doesn't need that. This needs to be surgical, but at the same time, make a point. Kendra seems to read my mind, because before I can say anything, she speaks up. "If you don't mind, I've got an idea."

I lift an eyebrow, waving for her to continue. "Go ahead."

"The way this needs to be handled . . . it needs to send a statement that takes you and Sarah out of consideration forever," Kendra says. "The key word is *statement*. You sent a big one with the way Jacob Waters died, but this needs to be different. Going after these fuckers with blazing guns like it's a fucking action movie won't do it."

I nod, impressed. She's always impressed me, not only as a badass whom I wouldn't want to cross, but even more than that, she's scary smart. She's studied The Art of War so much that she could probably write a pretty creative addendum with ideas that General Tzu never even considered. "I like it. Go on."

"You need something different. Something that not only takes Sarah off anyone's radar, but that will strike fear into the hearts of anyone considering stepping up in Jacob's absence."

Marcus and I look at each other, liking what we hear. Still, I'm feeling the urge to get things rolling. "Fast forward to the point, Kendra."

"These fuckers are cocky, think they're untouchable because Jacob always kept them close. But they're not, definitely not. And there's one man who can strike fear in the hearts of everyone in this city. Joe Strauss. Make a statement and have him go in covertly, one silent between the eyes, while they sleep peacefully in their own little beds at home, thinking they're safe and sound. One night, three hits, and by daybreak, word on the street will be out that anyone who opposes Ryker or thinks about getting a little too close to Sarah isn't safe anywhere, anytime. Nobody wants Joe after them. He's the fucking Grim Reaper, coming in like smoke you can't escape from."

I'm not surprised an idea like this would come from Kendra. It's brilliant, efficient, and absolutely on point. "Sounds good, for the most part. But I'd make one change."

"What's that?" Marcus asks.

I flex my hand, the knuckles on my right hand cracking like firecrackers in the suddenly still air of the warehouse office. "Viktor is mine. I have to be the one who does it. I'll send a final message. I might be moving out of the game, but that doesn't mean I've forgotten who and what I am. For the other two, call Joe and set it up. It needs to be soon—hell, even tonight if he can arrange it by then. I want this answered and done with before Sarah's bruises even change color. And Kendra? Thank you."

I leave Marcus and Kendra to make the arrangements. I hold my hand out to Sarah, and we leave the warehouse, getting into the waiting car so the guard can drive us home. She's silent the whole time, probably lost in thought and still recovering from the day's trauma. "Don't worry, babe, we'll be home soon."

When we get up to the penthouse, Sarah goes directly back to our bedroom, lying down silently. I sit lightly on the edge of the bed, not wanting to disturb her. Other than that half-smile, her face didn't move the entire time we were in the warehouse. I watch her for a moment, realizing how lucky I am that she's okay today. It could've been so much worse. I'll never forget the way my stomach dropped when Marcus came rushing in this afternoon like there were demons on his tail, telling me the news. Thankfully, she was found by a cop who works for us, and his first call was to my brother.

Sarah's my priority. I've got to keep her safe, away from

all the craziness that running this city entails. I lay down behind her, curling my body around hers, holding her close. "I promise," I whisper into her hair as I feel her trembles slowly ebb, "I promise I will keep you safe from now on. Whatever it takes."

"I know," Sarah whispers, reaching up to hold my hand. "I just worry it'll never be over. After this guy, who's to say there won't be another?"

"There won't be another after this," I say, knowing I might be lying even as I say it. Still, I have to keep hoping that I can get out, that Sarah's fears aren't true.

As her breathing deepens in the silence and I feel her slip off to sleep, I say a silent prayer thanking whatever god is listening for keeping her safe today.

CHAPTER 23

I look in the mirror, pushing back the uncertainty that's been haunting me the past three days since Viktor attacked me. There's still some bruising, but the puffiness is just about gone.

The first night was the worst. Ryker's sporting a bruise too after a PTSD nightmare had me lash out blindly in my sleep and nail him in the eye with an elbow. If I ever needed reminding that Ryker is different from Jacob, it was his reaction to that. He never even raised his voice. He just brushed it off and did his best to calm me down.

It's been like that the past three days. He's doted on me, nursed me, and been the perfect man for me. When Marcus or anyone else comes by, he has them talk in the living room, never excluding me but also giving me privacy if I don't want to listen in.

Still, I've been going stir-crazy in the apartment. Yesterday, I worked up the nerve to go down to the basement with Ryker as he exercised, but finally, this morning, I've had enough.

"So what do you want to do?" Ryker asks me as I come out of the bedroom in a plain scoop-neck tank top and jeans. His eyes flicker down to my cleavage, but in another sign that Ryker's wonderful, he doesn't say anything. He's being supportive but giving me space, waiting for me show that I'm ready before he tries to be intimate.

"I need to get out of here," I say, surprising him. "I can't spend the rest of my life holing up in this apartment like some sort of modern-day Howard Hughes. I want to go see the building that the Foundation's looking at renovating."

Ryker gives me a relieved smile and nods. "Great. You don't mind if you're escorted, though?" he asks, but it's pretty clear I'm not leaving his sight without security.

I shake my head. "Of course. That's fine and definitely for the best right now. Think you can ask Kendra? A little bit of girl time, and I think you've done more than enough to have earned a little bit of guy time. Go hang out with your brother, have a cheeseburger or something."

"I think we'll do more than that, but I'm sure Kendra would be happy to be your bodyguard today," Ryker replies. He gets on his phone, and about two hours later, the elevator dings as Marcus and Kendra arrive.

"Well, you two look comfy as hell," Kendra says, spying Ryker and me sprawled out on the couch. "Someday, I need to retire or something, get cuddle time like that."

"First, you gotta have someone to cuddle with," Marcus replies, and she gives him a smirk that makes Marcus blush slightly.

"So, how have you been?" Kendra asks me, sitting down. I can see the print of the gun tucked inside her pants pocket, and she glances down, adjusting.

"Ready to get out of here, do something productive," I reply. "How's things for you guys?"

Kendra gives Ryker a questioning look, obviously asking if she should speak freely in front of me. Ryker gives it right back, then glances at me. "It's your decision."

I shake my head, leaning forward. "I'm tired of ducking out. Guys, I need to hear it. Good, bad, or ugly. I've come to accept that the man I love is a criminal. I don't care what the law sees him as, and what you guys are doing right now . . . it might be against the law, but it's not wrong."

Ryker's eyes glow with warmth and love, and Kendra looks impressed as she gives me another evaluating look.

"Joe did his recon and then went into action last night,"

Kendra says as she leans forward. "Dezzie and Sam were taken out at their hangouts in typical Joe style."

"What, exactly, does that mean?" I ask curiously.

"He's our wet work guy. They were barely in the morgue before the word got out on the streets. This morning, the rats are scattering. Even our guys are pledging loyalty again, just in case, so that they don't meet Joe."

Marcus speaks up for the first time. "Yeah, I've been soothing scared big-ass dudes all damn morning. But really, the overall effect is what we expected. Jacob's network, other than Viktor, is one hundred percent dismantled. Our grip on the city is stronger than ever, and everyone knows we'll go full-throttle if needed. Even some of the holdout neutrals like Jacob's cops have reached out through their own channels to make it very clear they don't want to piss us off."

"Tell Chief Matthews we appreciate the gesture of friendship," I reply after a moment. I lean back, dark hilarity bubbling up through me as I start to laugh. Ryker reaches over, taking my hand, worried I might be pushed too far by this.

"Sarah, honey, it had to be done. I'm sorry. I know this isn't the life you want, but I had to do this. Please understand."

I realize he thinks I'm upset about the two deaths, some meek mouse cowering from the scary world around her. I understand, really. The past three nights, I've averaged about four hours of sleep per night, and not a lot of it being very restful. But I'm strong too, and I steel my gaze at him.

"Ryker, fuck that. I'm not upset you had those men killed. There's just one more thing. Kendra said Dezzie and Sam, but what about Viktor? The job's not done yet."

Ryker's eyes burn as my meaning soaks through his surprise, and he nods. "Are you sure?"

I reach across, grabbing his hand. "He could've killed me, and if I'd been physically able to, I would've killed him myself. Because he's more than just a threat to me, but a threat to you, to your brother, and to the people I care about. There's a saying I learned back when I was acting, and I always felt silly repeating it. But it makes sense now. *Ride or die.* And I know you live by that. So thank you. Thank you for doing what I couldn't do and keeping not just me safe, but the whole city."

I move in to kiss Ryker, and I can feel his relief as he covers my mouth with his. In an instant, the fire ignites and I'm nearly straddling his waist when I hear someone loudly clearing their throat. I turn, blushing when I see Kendra and Marcus watching us, Kendra looking amused and Marcus looking like he'd rather be anywhere else in the world right this second. Pulling back, I grin sheepishly. "Sorry, guys, got a little carried away."

Marcus laughs, shrugging. "Quite all right, although I

could do without seeing my ugly as hell brother like that. Not again."

The boys grin at each other, and I catch a glimpse of what they were probably like as kids, always mischievous and getting into trouble. "Yeah, well," Ryker says, patting my hip, "I think Sarah and Kendra have a visit to make?"

"We do," Kendra says, bouncing to her feet. "Don't worry, she'll be safe."

I give Ryker a quick goodbye peck on the lips to avoid any more temptation or awkwardness before grabbing my purse and getting in the elevator with Kendra. The doors close, and she gives me a grin. "So . . . ride or die?"

I giggle. The way she says it makes me laugh, and I nod. "Um, yeah. Hey, got a question. Who's Joe?"

For the rest of the ride down the elevator, I'm in awe as Kendra tells me about the junior high school teacher-slash-hitman, thinking surely, she's joking, but apparently, he's the most incognito scary dude in the city.

"Oh, Joe did have one request for this job. He's apparently a big fan and appreciates what you're looking at doing with the Broken Angel Foundation. He's weird like that, ruthless but with a soft side too. He wondered if you'd make an appearance at his school and give a talk about healthy relationships and what to do if you're in an abusive one. He thinks it'd be a good intro for his students to hear before they start dating in high school."

I'm in awe that someone wants to hear me talk and thinks I'd have a positive impact. I'm sure not an expert on that topic, but I do know what it's like to be in an unhealthy relationship. I nod excitedly. "Absolutely. I'd love to."

Kendra grins, cranking the engine on her car. "Good. I gotta tell you, though, Joe's not the only person in the life who's glad about your Foundation."

Something in her tone gives me pause. "What's your story?" I ask. "I mean, tell me to fuck off if you want. I won't be offended. But you know, you're like the only female friend I have. We're supposed to share this stuff, right?"

Kendra pulls out into the street, her mouth going tight. "Someday, Sarah . . . maybe I'll have the guts to tell you. Until then, just know I've been forced to stare into the abyss long enough that it knows me inside and out too."

CHAPTER 24

*T*he night air is getting slightly nippy. We're in that transition time of the year when the days can have you in t-shirts and your evenings in coats. It's a good night for what I want to do.

I know I can't trust that the fear of using Joe is going to stop everyone who opposes me, especially the cops who might be still be looking for a way to take me down. It's always a balancing act with them. They do, technically, have the law on their side.

I thought it over obsessively, and I was tempted to take Viktor out the same way I took out Jacob. I mean, killing two men with knives in their own homes is pretty damn iconic. It'd send a message, kinda like my signature, with the kills.

But this needs something different, so I decided on this course of action. It's not common in urban gang fights, mainly because it's so damn difficult. Compared to the number of idiots who just want to do drive-bys and spray rounds all over the street, sniping is a relatively long-lost art.

Thankfully, I've learned that art. Part of it was Dad, who would get me and Marcus out of the city when he could. He'd take us up to the mountains and out into the green hills, where we'd have to fend for ourselves. This was before Mom left, so it was sort of a male bonding time for us.

I'm teaming with Marcus and borrowing a tactic used by others. Our vehicle is nondescript, a blue Tahoe that looks like just about any of a thousand others around the city. If anyone got close enough to look through the tinted windows, they'd wonder why the back seats are folded down. But nobody's going to get that close.

While Joe was scoping out his targets, Marcus has had everyone looking for Viktor. Finally, a call from one of our cops at the airport reported that he's been holing up at a private 'airline' that runs charter flights out of the city. Smart move, really. People don't like causing shit around the airport. It gets the Feds involved.

But he has to leave the airport eventually, and we've been ready and waiting to get the call that he's on the move. I know his destination because I know where he keeps his liquid funds, in the safe at a strip club a half-mile from the airport that was one of Jacob's lesser-known 'investments'. The Blue Room isn't the most famous club in town, but that's because it doesn't advertise like its brethren. It mostly serves as a business front to launder money, but the 'one-night shows' of some of the most famous names in the porn industry are the stuff of legend, and the normal girls who work there are some of the freakiest around. But the girls won't be Viktor's reason for going there. He's gonna do a grab-and-go, get his cash and hustle back to the airport to get his ass out of town. He's such a pussy, stirring up shit but unwilling to finish it. "You know, I visited here once," Marcus says as we wait in the corner of the parking lot next to a few of the workers' cars. "Did I ever tell you about that?"

"You know, you haven't," I reply as I edge myself into the backseat area before turning around. "If you had, I would have kicked your ass. When was that?"

"Three days after my eighteenth birthday," Marcus says, checking the mirrors and the small video screen in the dash while I uncase my rifle. "Downtown Bootsy and Frankie Dawlish brought me, said they'd make sure I was inducted into manhood properly while you were kept busy. They lent me a suit and all the trimmings to make sure that I looked the part and didn't catch the attention of management."

I suppress a growl. Those assholes should know better. "Well, you can tell me about it another time. It's go time."

I make my final preparation, removing a piece of glass from the rear window that'll be totally replaced by tomorrow. To the outside, it looks like just a broken window. We've taped a piece of clear plastic over the hole. I slide behind my rifle. It's a modified Remington 700P. I chose it for a reason, though, because it's the same type of weapon used by the city's SWAT snipers. Instant courtroom reasonable doubt.

We know Viktor's in there. One of our crew watched him go in an hour ago. What kind of asshole on the run takes an hour strip club break as he's getting his go-funds? This guy, apparently. I hope he enjoys that BJ because it'll be his last. Now it's just a waiting game.

I sit, using the firing blocks we've set up to keep the rifle at just the right height. With no flash or sound suppressor, it's going to be loud in the Tahoe when I fire, but it'll be safer this way.

My spine is starting to ache as the minutes drag by. Sitting cross-legged with half my ass on the folded down seat isn't recommended by any chiropractor. Just as I do some light twists to make sure I'm not going to be too tight, Marcus speaks up. "Door."

I raise the rifle, looking through the scope as the front door to The Blue Room opens and three men emerge. Two of them are obviously bodyguards, typical thug-gish-looking meatheads who get by more on their sheer bulk and intimidation than real skills.

In the middle, slightly behind them, is Viktor. It's a sign both of his arrogance and of his bodyguards' limited skills that I have a sightline on him at all. Totally unprofessional.

It's mistakes like this that show why you could never be the King, I think as I push the safety off and take the final breath before I fire. I let it half out, waiting as everything comes into place. When it does, I stroke the sensitive trigger, and a single hollow-point round flies. I lose my view of Viktor in the blur of recoil through my scope, but when I can see again, both bodyguards look panicked and Viktor's down.

Message sent.

"Let's go."

CHAPTER 25

RYKER

The past two and a half months have felt like a whirlwind of activity, taking over our entire lives, but really, it's just been the setup for The Broken Angel Foundation. Just helping Nikolas with everything involved in getting the gala going has been hard work, but Sarah's also been busting her ass trying to get as much done on the shelter as possible. She's going to make her goal, with a grand opening scheduled for December fifteenth, just in time for Christmas.

The city has settled quite nicely in the two months since we took care of Jacob's last loyal followers. Crews are selling, girls on the street are safe, docks and airport are running, and Marcus and I have had meetings with all the major players to ease any doubts they had about our leadership. We've been selling it as a dual-headed leadership, and everyone seems to understand that, as brothers, we're a package deal. They're not gonna complain as long as everything is running smoothly anyway.

I shake my head as I think of Marcus. He's been great in his new role, and my transition to retirement from the game has been smoother than I could have ever imagined. A lot of it, of course, has been Kendra. Now officially his Chief Lieutenant, she hasn't let a single thing slip at the street level now that Marcus has to look at the overall scene. If anything, things have tightened up. All it took was Kendra's kicking the one guy's ass who thought to challenge her leadership to remind everyone that her rep is earned . . . with their blood.

I still get a vibe between them that makes me curious, although both of them swear that there's nothing going on between them. We'll see. Right now, I'm just happy to be the man behind the curtain.

Standing in the corner of the hotel ballroom, I can't really believe we've pulled it all off. Sure, Nikolas has hired a small army to do what they can, and I'll admit I've pulled a few strings myself, but the success of tonight totally rests on one woman's shoulders. Sarah's been a force of nature, animated by a passion that fills her to overflowing. Not that we've ever had a problem letting off overflowing passions.

Sarah's flitting around the room like a six-foot-tall butterfly behind Nikolas, moving and adjusting flowers and forks, just to have Nikolas move them back. She's nervous about tonight, but she doesn't need to be. The gala is going to be a success, and it'll help fund the shelter along with Sarah's contributions. People know and love her as an actress, and the whole city knows she's mine, so they'll be coming out in droves tonight to show support.

Besides, she's got a great lineup for the gala. I didn't even know it, but a former co-star on her show has started up a headline-grabbing pop band, and they're playing the gala for free in between concerts.

Still, Nikolas looks like he's about to lose his shit, so as he and Sarah get a little closer to me, I sneak up behind her, taking her by the arm and spinning her around. She whirls, surprised. "Hey!"

"Hey yourself," I say with a grin. "Calm down. You're making Nikolas nervous, and everything is already perfect."

Nikolas gives me a grateful wave of his hand as Sarah takes a deep breath, relaxing in my arms, "I know, but I don't know what to do with myself. People will be here soon, and I just want it all to go well."

"Come on, I have an idea," I say as I let go of her enough to take her hand and lead her out of the ball-room and down the hall to one of the powder rooms. Glancing up and down the hall, I open the door and lead her inside, pulling her close as soon as we're alone. I wrap a perfectly curled tendril of hair she has dangling down her cheek around my finger, looking into her eyes and smiling. "Have I told you how gorgeous you look tonight? This dress is spectacular on you."

In fact, the Vera Wang dress she's wearing tonight has been the focus of several pointed conversations. While it looks stunning on her curves, it has a low back that shows off the scarred lines crisscrossing her spine. I think it makes her look even stronger and sends a message that's more powerful than anything she's going to say when she makes a speech later tonight, but she was hesitant. She was sure it was a horrendous choice, that it'd take away attention from the Foundation, but in the end, I convinced her that her scars showed that she survived. She got out.

I think it was her acceptance of her scars that has done more to help her with her PTSD than anything else. Well, maybe that and Kendra teaching her how to be a badass fighter, too. I can appreciate that, but right now, I'm holding a tender, nervous Sarah who needs comfort . . . and maybe some distraction.

"Thank you," she says as I stroke her back. She shivers, and I can feel her nipples start to harden inside her dress. "Mmm . . . you were right. I feel exposed in a good way."

I cover her mouth with a kiss, our tongues tangling as she relaxes in my arms. Nibbling at her ear, I lick the curve, and she tilts her head, giving me more access. "Turn around," I half growl, half whisper as I assist her, my hands on her hips and helping her face the mirrored makeup counter. I dip down to sprinkle little kisses and licks down her back, and she instinctively arches for me.

"What are you doing? The gala . . ." Sarah moans breathlessly as I lick and suckle on her neck and along her spine. I kiss her deepest scar like I always do, renewing my promise to her and to myself that she'll never, ever have to face the pain that she did before.

"Giving you exactly what you need," I growl as my hands reach down and start to lift up the silky fabric of her dress. It's sexy and stretchy enough that it hugs her curves but slides up her legs so easily. Kneeling down, Sarah bends over almost unconsciously as I lift her dress past the curve of her ass, kissing the dimples at the base of her spine. "You're freaking out, so I'm helping you relax and keeping you out of Nikolas's way. You're mine right now. The gala can have you in a few minutes after you're glowing from coming all over my tongue."

I trace her inner thigh up toward the edge of her panties, slipping them to the side to find her already wet for me. Sarah gasps, trying to argue even as she bends over more, and her breath catches in her throat. "We can't . . . shouldn't . . . I need to . . . mmm . . . oh, God . . . lock the door, please?"

I grin, getting to my feet and quickly throwing the latch on the door before reassuming my position on my knees and sliding Sarah's panties back to the side. I stroke over her soft lips before dipping inside her heat, coating my fingers in her honey and slipping up to her clit, slowly circling to spread her juices. I draw back, looking at the glistening moisture on my fingers, and slowly lick them clean. "Mmm, I need more of you. Spread your legs for me, Sarah. I promise you, you're going to love this."

She obeys, placing her forearms on the counter and pressing her hips back, opening for me. I have a close-up view of her perfect little lips, covered in her glistening need. I press against the button of her clit, tapping it gently as I bend forward, burying my face between her ass cheeks and stroking my tongue over her pussy.

"Oh, fuck," Sarah groans, pushing back into me as I lick and suck on her pussy while teasing her clit, alternating feather-light touches and little love taps. I press my tongue deeper into her, driving her crazy until she's grinding her hips against my face, desperate for more. I pull my mouth back to slide two fingers deep inside her, curling my fingers as I rise up to circle her waist with my other hand, holding her up as her knees shake. I curl my fingers against her front wall as I tease her clit with my thumb, sending her into total sensory overload. Sarah bucks against me, fucking herself on my fingers, and I lean forward, kissing her ear again. "That's it, take what you need. Get there, my love. I want you to come all over my fingers and let it all go. Just be free."

Her body tenses for a moment as her eyes find mine in the mirror, but then she's flying, her body clenching around my fingers as she shudders. "Fuck, Ry. Yes!" she gasps, collapsing so that she's totally given herself over to me, held up only by my arm around her middle.

I hum, nuzzling her neck as I pull my fingers free, bringing them to my mouth to suck her honey clean again. I want to have her taste on my tongue and her smell on my hand all night, knowing that as everyone else congratulates her and schmoozes with her, she's all mine.

After a moment, she regains her feet, turning around to look me in the eyes. I grin, pretty damn proud of myself. "You relaxed now, babe? Ready to greet the masses?"

Sarah tucks a lock of hair behind her ear, shaking her head and smirking. "Definitely feeling better, thank you. What about you, though?"

I reach down, adjusting the throbbing, hot length of my cock in my tuxedo pants, and grin. "We'll handle that later. Tonight's all about you, how fucking wonderful you are, and what you're going to be able to show the world. So don't worry about me."

I help her get her panties and dress situated and offer her my arm as I unlock the door. We step out of the bathroom like it's totally normal, and I pause to give her a kiss on the cheek. "Miss Desjardins, you are the most beautiful woman in the world."

"Mr. Johns, you sure do make me feel that way."

CHAPTER 26

I step out of my office and into the warm spring air. Easter's just around the corner, and as winter's bite has faded and spring has emerged, I've never been busier. Or happier. I have a million things on my mind, but first is knowing that some caffeine is just what I need to keep rolling on this busy day. The Broken Angel Foundation has been a total success, and while I'm sad that our clients have been through hell, I'm glad we're able to help them get back on a happier path.

The gala was a night I'll never forget. The room was packed, and I don't know if it was the speech I gave, the band, Nikolas's party planning, or just pure luck, but it seemed everyone showed up with a checkbook that overflowed with zeroes. In one night, we not only secured enough funds to totally renovate our original location, but also enough to break ground on a second shelter on the other side of town, doubling our bed count. With some of the corporate benefactors we've gathered, I've even started looking at setting up a unit of family suites. So far, the mayor's been on board, and when he hasn't . . . well, as the song goes, *Damn, it feels good to be a gangster.*

It's been a gift to give these families a safe place to sleep, even hiring several off-duty police officers whom Marcus recommended to keep everything secure in the evenings and overnight. Ryker was happy about that because while we haven't had any issue with Jacob's old cronies since he 'nailed' Viktor, as the streets called it, this is still a large city that will always be ripe for criminal activity, so he worries about my safety.

I tease him that he only spends so much time worrying about me because he's bored, but that's not really true. With Marcus busy running the city and Ryker being more of a background man in their deal, he has been instrumental with running the foundation. It's amazing how we can wake in each other's arms, ride together to the office, work all day as we sneak an occasional long lunch break in, and then ride back home together to do it all over again the next day. I love getting to spend my time with him, both of us passionate to make a positive change for the city and the families who live within the foundation's care.

I don't have time right now to think about Ryker. I've got a very important debt to pay. Heading down to the parking garage, I have to smile when I see Kendra waiting for me. "Asked Marcus if I could be your driver today. He said no problem."

"You keep driving for me, people are gonna think you're not a badass anymore," I tease, jumping in the back of the black Lincoln as Kendra gets behind the wheel. While she's dressed more professionally than what I normally see her in, I know she's armed. And there's no way she'd fit in some of the boardrooms I've done presentations in over the past six months. "So you doing okay?"

"You know it," Kendra says. She chuckles as I fidget around in the back seat, stripping out of my office clothes for what I normally wear for these sorts of things. Kendra knows, but she still likes to tease me. "Hey, if you wanna take off your clothes for money, I know a place—"

"Just drive," I mockingly growl as she laughs. It takes us about thirty minutes with downtown traffic to reach our destination, a nondescript squat brick building in one of the middle-class areas of town. I look around as we pull into the visitor's parking slot, chuckling. "You know, I never would have imagined he'd work here."

"Hey, the man's got a cover story that's damn near airtight," Kendra says. "Besides, it's gotta be cool to be able to get away and do something to balance those karmic scales. I'll wait in the office, though, if you don't mind. Me and formal education don't exactly have a good history."

"Why's that?" I ask as I get out, Kendra following behind me just as she's supposed to as we approach the doorway. "Too worried about the guys in class?"

"Nah, but after kicking my seventh grade math teacher in the nuts . . . well, I kinda got a reputation," Kendra says. She stops at the door, looking at the metal detector. "Damn."

"Don't worry, I'll wave you through," comes a soft spoken voice from the office. There's a buzz, and the two of us step through, approaching the check-in desk where I see a balding, slightly overweight man with thick glasses that are just this side of Coca-Cola bottles. He gives me a soft smile, offering his hand. "Miss Desjardins, it's a pleasure to see you, as always."

"Hi, Mr. Strauss. It's good to see you again," I reply as Kendra and Joe give each other the respectful nod that comes from the other side of this unassuming man's life. I've come to recognize a lot of it over the past six months, and I know that without even saying a word, Joe's saying he'll take care of me while Kendra's saying she holds him responsible for anything that happens. I give them a moment, and when Joe turns his eyes back to me, I smile. "Shall we?"

"Of course," Joe says, leading me down the hallway. "I

have to admit, the students are excited. Now that your show's getting new airplay on one of the local stations, you're . . . well, let's just say I've had to tell a few of my more interested boys to tone down the comments."

I chuckle, shaking my head. "Joe, we both know boys will say stupid shit."

"True," Joe says as we turn a corner, "but that doesn't mean we can't show them the right way to do things. I have to say, thank you. I thought you'd stop after that first speech at the student government event."

"Most of the time, it's not the class presidents we need to reach out to," I say softly, pausing in the hallway. "It's the kids who never get within sniffing distance of that sort of recognition. The kids who've already seen it modeled for them by their own parents or, God forbid, are already caught up in the cycle themselves."

"You ever know someone caught up in it and you need my help, give me a call," Joe says, his voice still quiet but colder. "No charge."

"I'll pass that along," I say. We get going again, emerging into the school gymnasium just as the principal gives me a rousing welcome. I take the microphone from her with a nod and a hug before stepping back and looking around at the six hundred faces watching me as I clear my throat.

"Thank you, Garfield Junior High, for having me today. I'm sure some of you are wondering just why I'm here.

It's not about acting. That's another life for me. Instead, I'd like to talk about something that started just after I stopped acting for the cameras and started acting for my life."

There's always this moment as I set the microphone down on the small table that the school's prepared for me, and I untuck the plain black dress shirt that I wear for my speeches. When I pick up the microphone again, I can see a few people sitting forward, curious. I get right down to it, and I reach for the first button on my blouse, and I can practically feel three hundred boys' eyes half pop out of their skulls as I begin unbuttoning my top. A few people look shocked, but the principal knows what I'm going to do. I've already sent her pictures. When I reach the last button, I pull my shirt off with a bit of flair, revealing the swimsuit I wear underneath. It's specially made, with a low enough cut that the biggest scar on my chest is visible. I set my shirt aside and pick up the microphone again.

"Let me tell you not about my life in front of the camera, but the acting I had to do after the lights were off and the man I married carved these on my skin."

"So, how'd it go?" Kendra asks as I get back in the car.

"If you can believe it, Joe cried when he gave me a thank you hug," I tell her. "Oh, and if we ever need his services in a situation relating to the Foundation, he said it's free of charge."

Kendra glances over, nodding in appreciation. I'm sitting up front this time. I only ride in the back with her if I have to. I enjoy this casual, friendly setup more. "So, where to now?"

"Back to the grind," I say with a laugh. "You sure you don't want to volunteer down at the Foundation?"

"You kidding me?" Kendra says as she pulls out of the parking lot and we head back downtown. "Hate to tell you, but most criminals are that way because they like getting a lot of money for not a lot of hours working. And you want me to just give my work away for free?"

"Damn right, I do," I reply. "I'm not asking Ryker's crewmember. I'm asking my friend."

Kendra glances over, shaking her head. She says nothing until we're all the way back in the parking garage and she puts the Lincoln in park. "I'll see you Monday morning then," she says quietly. "Just promise me that I don't have to get all dressed up or anything. You make me wear a skirt, and I'm quitting on your ass."

I lean over, giving her a hug. "You can wear anything you want. Ride or die, babe."

She claps me on the back, and we get out, Kendra walking me to the elevator before stopping. "I'd go up, but I promised Marcus I'd get some other things looked after. I'll stop by the penthouse sometime over the weekend, if you're free."

I give her a wave and take the elevator up, my exhaustion hitting me like a ton of bricks. I realize I'd skipped my earlier coffee dose and head for the break room as soon as the elevator doors open. I'm hustling so much as I turn the corner that I almost crash into Ryker as he turns the corner, catching me as his large hands wrap around my upper arms when I stumble.

"Hey, babe, where you headed so fast? How was the speech?"

"Coffee. Must have coffee," I reply, faking a pretty good zombie moaning growl, and he laughs at me.

"I've got you. You know, if you ever want to go back to acting, I bet *The Walking Dead* would love to have you as a guest star with that imitation. C'mon." He grabs my hand, walking toward the kitchen. Grabbing two cups of joe, we head out to the garden.

Yes, the Broken Angel Foundation has a garden. The building is built in an octagonal shape, and there was no way I was going to waste that big open area in the middle. In the center of the garden is our mascot, a gorgeous marble angel standing seven feet tall. The garden is full of flowering trees and bushes, little pops of colorful flowers, rows of veggies, and private sitting areas for people to escape to when they need a moment alone. It's peaceful and one of my favorite things about the whole facility. Settling in my favorite lounge chair,

I take a long, slow sip, the fog clearing from my eyes enough to realize he's staring at me, his eyes virtually twinkling.

No way. I haven't told anyone my secret, not even Kendra when I had the opportunity earlier today. I mean, I just found out yesterday. But . . . does he know already? There's no way he knows.

Finally, I can't stand it anymore. "You're looking at me like a kid who just got a puppy for Christmas. What's up?"

Ryker sets his coffee down, almost vibrating with excitement as he reaches out and takes my hand. "I heard back. They said yes. The league agreed, and now I'm the coach. Hey, batter, batter, sa-wing, batter."

His grin is so big, lighting up his face with joy, that I can imagine what he looked like as a boy. He'd come up with the idea of a Little League baseball team for the kids staying at the shelter, but there were a ton of challenges. First was the fact that so many of the city kids have never played baseball. Basketball? Sure, they've been hooping since they could walk. But baseball takes space, and in this city, that's at a premium.

But Ryker's been insistent. "It'll make sure every kid starts off with a fair chance," he said when he explained it to the Foundation board, "and it'll give every kid a chance to feel real grass. It might be the biggest chunk of grass these kids have seen in their entire lives up to this point, and that's not right. So let's start making it right."

It convinced the board, but it was a logistical difficulty to get approval because players have to be on the roster for the whole season and we have a rotating list of kids depending on when their families move in and move on. But Ryker's personality and force of will are undeniable, and within days of announcing it to the shelter families, Ryker had enough kids interested to start holding practices. Convincing the league took a bit more persuasion, but with all of his resources, Ryker's a convincing person.

"So you made them an offer they couldn't refuse?" I joke, and Ryker laughs, leaning back in his chair.

"What can I say? They respected my point of view."

I can't hold back my excitement, getting out of my chair and sitting in his lap. I give him a huge hug, squeezing as tight as I can. I'm so damn proud of him. "I'm so happy for you. You know, you really should think about running for mayor someday. This town could use someone like you running it."

He chuckles, and we stay wrapped in each other's arms, relaxing back into the lounger. Ryker absently runs his fingers up and down my arm, leaving goosebumps, both of us enjoying the moment of calm in our new busy daily schedules.

After a few minutes, he kisses my shoulder softly. "Sarah, thank you. This life . . . it's not what I ever thought I'd have, but you gave me more than I ever thought I deserved. You're amazing."

I smile, turning to look at him and stroke his face. "Ryker, you saved me—not just physically, but mentally, emotionally, and spiritually. I had almost given up. That run where you caught me was it for me. I was getting away or I was gonna die trying. You have kept me safe and taught me that love does exist, and it is beautiful, not ugly, controlling cruelty. With you, I thrive. Thank you."

I lean forward, and our lips meet in a kiss, sweet at first, but as always, our fire lights easily, and we kiss with passion and abandon. After a moment, Ryker ends the kiss, pulling back. "Wait. I wasn't done. You're more than I deserve, more than I dreamed, but I want more."

Ryker helps me out of the chair, getting out himself to kneel alongside it. My breath hitches in my throat and my heart stops as I think, *Is he doing what I think he's doing?*

He is. Oh, my God, he is. Ryker takes my hand in his, kissing my knuckles with a butterfly soft kiss before looking up into my eyes. It's hard to see. I'm already tearing up, but I have to hear the words. "Sarah, you are my Rygirl. Forever in my heart, the only person I will love. I promise you, I will do everything I can, give everything I am, to give you a home that is safe, a family that cares for you, and to give you every happiness that exists in this world every day for the rest of our lives. Sarah, will you marry me?"

I'm so filled with joy that it bursts out in tears as I nod, barely able to say yes, but he seems to understand. He swoops up, pulling me into his arms and hugging me tight. And I know I'm right where I should be, safe and happy in his arms, in his heart. Laughing, he twirls me around until I beg him to stop. I look up at him.

"So, uh . . . Ry? I have some news too. You're gonna be Coach, but you're also gonna be . . . Daddy. I'm pregnant."

His jaw drops as his eyes go wide, and he takes a step back, catching his balance as the news hits him. "Are you serious? Oh, my God. Daddy. You're pregnant."

He's rambling, obviously a bit in shock, but then his gaze locks on me as he pulls me in tight, swaying back and forth a little. I feel a little shudder in his chest, and his voice cracks. "Sarah? Thank you for making me the happiest man alive. I love you so much."

I wrap my arms around him, laying my head on his shoulder. "I love you, too. Oh, and one last thing. You have to call Nikolas to tell him we need a wedding before I start showing. He's probably only got a couple of months, but he pulled off the gala that fast before, so hopefully, he can work some magic."

Ryker kisses my temple, laughter in his voice. "For you, we can definitely make some magic happen."

I know there's a thousand and one things still to do today. Knowing that makes me happy. But for right now, I just want to take a moment with my king, holding each other and swaying in the garden, surrounded by our hopes and dreams coming true.

Join my mailing list and receive 2 FREE ebooks!
You'll also be the first to know of new releases, sales, and giveaways.

PREVIEW: MR. FIXIT

BY LAUREN LANDISH

Cassie

*T*he blistering heat envelops me as I step outside with a glass of cold water in my hand. Immediately, the humidity makes my thin cotton tank top cling to my body even before I'm halfway down the steps.

"I get it, I get it," I mutter to myself, glancing up to the heavens. "I've been such a bad girl that I have to spend the summer living next door to the gates of hell. Doesn't mean you have to throw in the mugginess too."

At least the weather's good for one thing, I think as I feel a droplet of sweat trickle down the back of my thigh. I can barely stand to wear anything at all, so I've spent most of the past few days in nothing but crop tops and Daisy Dukes. Sure, I might be looking just a tad bit skanky, but I think I can pull it off. And it's done wonders for my tan.

I hear the buzzing of the small gasoline motor, and I come around the corner of the house, knowing what I'll find. After a delay in getting some of the materials that we need, Caleb and I decided to tackle something else. A friend of his was willing to let us borrow his big riding lawnmower, so we're tackling the one-acre space behind the house, taking it from a jungle to a half-tamed space. We'll worry about making it a lawn later, but today's all about at least getting it so that I'm not worried about snakes or other creepy crawlies if I want to take a walk back here.

Caleb and I have been working together all morning to try and get the lawn done, alternating between driving the mower and using the other tools. We've been through six gallons of gas in the big mower, but the ten huge bags of cut grass stand as a monument to the amount of work we've accomplished. But now, he insists on running the weed whacker, saying my bare legs are in danger. The way he keeps looking at my legs and ass, I'd say he's the one in danger . . . and that's just the way I like it.

"Do you need some wa—" I yell, but the words freeze in my throat at the sight in front of me. Caleb's peeled off his shirt while I've been inside, leaving him in just a pair of jeans that hugs his lean hips like a glove, and I get a full view of the long muscles of his back and the swell of his arms and shoulders as he shuts off the motor. Just looking at the sweat glistening on his tanned skin makes my internal temperature ratchet up a few more degrees, and I'm tempted to drink half the glass of water myself. I'm burning up inside.

"Hey," he says, turning all the way toward me and shrugging off the gas trimmer. Watching his chest and arms flex with easy strength and the bead of sweat that trickles down his pecs before coursing its way over the deep ridges of his abs has me gasping for air.

I've always known that Caleb was a fine, sexy specimen of manhood. But the recent change in our relationship has me looking at him differently. I'm shocked at how turned on he makes me. These past few days, I've noticed him not as an opponent, not as a playmate, but as a man. And no matter how much I want to deny it, I want him with every fiber of my being.

Why couldn't I see this before? It makes sense. From the moment I saw him, I wanted to beat him, to show him that I was worthy of his notice. Every mean trick I played on him, every time I've tried to show him up since we've started working together, it's always been to get his attention. Sometimes, I've been subtle, like with a slight joke or making sure I wore my thinnest bra today underneath my thinnest tank top. Other times, it's been as in your face as a bucket of water poured over his head. Yeah, I did that too.

And now, I can't deny it. I can't get enough of him.

The corner of Caleb's lips curl up into a cocky grin as

he watches me, and I realize I'm staring at him, the glass of ice water frozen in my hand. "You okay?"

I tear my eyes away from his sweaty abs. "Yeah, a bead of sweat just fell in my eye." I lie my ass off, trying to maintain at least a little bit of control of myself. I'm not quite that desperate that I want to fall on my back in the freshly mown grass and spread my legs, begging him to plow me. At least, not yet. I wipe at my eyes with the back of my hand, holding out the glass of cold water. "Here. You look like you need it."

Caleb reaches out and takes the glass from my hand, my eyes fixed on his Adam's apple as he downs half the glass, his throat making me even more breathless before he stops and gives me a curious look. "You sure about that?"

He steps closer, and he's so close I can feel the heat emanating from him, heat that has nothing to do with the blistering sun. I swear my internal thermometer is rising through the roof. Standing next to him, the only image I have in my head is of my entire head exploding like a cartoon thermometer, but I can't tear my eyes away from him.

"I'm sure," I finally reply, my voice husky. "How much more do you have to do?"

"Not much," Caleb admits, not looking anywhere but at me. "There's a few bushes that need trimmed, but that won't take long at all."

If you want to see a nicely trimmed bush, I've got one for you, I think, but instead, I nod. "Okay."

The sounds of the summer fade away as I watch him finish off his drink, a trickle of water running from the side of his mouth and down to his chest, making me want to lick the clear droplet off his skin. He licks his lips, and all I can imagine is feeling his hands, his lips, his tongue licking me that way, and I moan lightly, my thighs trembling with desire.

Caleb finishes the last bit from the glass before crunching one of the ice cubes that I'd put inside, smiling. "Delicious. Just what I needed."

Please, please, PLEASE run that ice cube over my nipples, I want to beg him, my heart pounding in my chest like a sexual drum. "Yeah. I was just going back inside. I was going to get that list of stuff for the bathr—"

Trying to keep my eyes in a safe place, I fail utterly. Every glance at Caleb makes me want him more, and I stammer, unable to find a single square inch of his body that doesn't leave my heart fluttering, my stomach twisting, and my pussy aching. Finally, in a desperate bid for keeping control, I turn to leave, but I freeze when I feel a powerful hand grab my wrist.

"What are you doing?" I gasp as Caleb pulls me back around, my body pressing against his. I can feel his heart pounding against my chest, and between his legs is a throbbing, thick heat that leaves my knees weak.

Caleb grins at me, his eyes twinkling in a way that I've

never seen before. "You didn't call me names like you normally do."

"Oh," I whimper weakly. "I just forgot. This heat has me burning up."

Caleb lowers his lips until I can feel his breath on my ear, and I whimper again, my nipples hardening inside my top. "I think you're burning up all right. And I know just what to do about it."

"Oh, is that so?" I ask as my hands clutch at the full, hard muscles on his chest.

"It is," he purrs, pressing himself into me. I can feel the rapidly hardening growth of his cock, and my legs seem to spread on their own to let him have access to me. I want him so damn badly I can taste him already.

He pulls me tighter, and I moan, unable to form words. He's got me right where he wants me. Caleb whispers in my ear, "You have a problem, and I have the tool for the job."

He grabs another one of the ice cubes from his glass, gently dropping the glass to the grass. I bite my lip as he brings the ice cube to my jawline, tracing the line and then letting the drops run down my neck. He dips his head down to lick at the river of drops from the quickly melting ice, humming in satisfaction.

"Mmm, even more refreshing than I thought. Are you cooled off now?"

Knowing it'll drive him crazy, I smirk and shake my

head. "Not even close. In fact, I might be even hotter now."

"We can't have that, now can we?" he says as he trails the little bit of remaining ice down toward my cleavage. I press my tits together, creating a little crevice for the water to puddle, and Caleb's eyes focus there. Moving his hands over mine, he cups my breasts together even higher, lowering his head to dip his tongue into the pool, lapping the water up and running his tongue along the upper crest of my breasts. My head falls back as I groan. The water gone now, he moves to slip the neckline of my tank down, giving him more access. Kissing down, he slurps my nipple into his mouth, swirling his tongue over the peaked tip. He's driving me crazy, and I know my panties are already soaked.

I'm this close to letting him take me right here in the backyard, whoever can see be damned, when I hear my phone blare out. *"Work hard, play hard."*

"Shit," I gasp, pushing away from Caleb and going over to his truck to grab my bag off the tailgate. My phone's still singing its digital ass off, and I know from the ringtone that it's work. I pull it out and see that it's Martha. "Fuck!"

"Well, that was sort of what I had in mind," Caleb teases, grabbing my hips from behind and pulling me closer, but I pull away before I can be swept away in the sexual passion coursing through me.

I hold up a finger to signal for him to hold on a second, answering the call. "Hey, Martha, what's up?"

Caleb realizes it's work and is professional enough to not do anything too naughty. Good boy. "Hey, Cass," Martha says. "I hope you're not waiting on me."

Oh, shit, I forgot . . . Martha is supposed to come to the house today. It's a good damn thing she didn't pull up just now or she would've gotten a bit more show than she'd planned on. "Oh, um, no, Martha, not at all," I quickly reply while trying not to facepalm myself. I've done that before, and it's not a good thing to do while you have your smartphone to your face. "Actually, we're just finishing up the yardwork. Why?"

"Well, I guess we're both lucky then," Martha says with a relieved sigh. "I was getting my hair done, and you know how the salon can get on the weekends. Is there any way you could meet me at the office in an hour instead of my driving out there?"

"Yeah, no problem," I say, relieved. "I'll see you there."

We hang up, and I turn to Caleb, who looks disappointed. "Sorry."

"Work?" he asks, and I'm counting the minutes in my head even as I look down. An hour. That means we have about ten minutes to . . .

No, stop it, dammit, I tell myself.

"Yeah, work. I promised Martha I'd go over some documents with her. She's gotta send them off Monday morning or else."

Caleb sighs but nods. "I understand. Well, at least I know I can make you lose all track of time."

I laugh, shaking my head. "Probably because you're so boring you put me to sleep."

"Is that what you call it when you scream my name and pass out? Boring. I'll remember that."

Want to read more of Caleb & Cassie's explosive antics? Get it HERE.

SNEAK PEEK: MATCHMAKER

BY LAUREN LANDISH

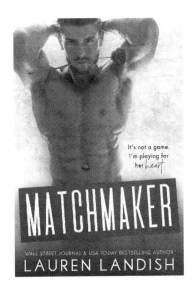

Coming Oct. 20th!

Hayden

*J*t's mad early for breakfast, but since ending our date, I've felt like I can't get my mind off of Emily. As I'm rounding a corner, I see her, dressed in a beautiful white dress, her long, sexy legs on display, heading into a door ahead. A grin spreads across my face as I rush up the hallway and sneak in behind her.

I try to be quiet as I come through the door, but Emily immediately senses my presence and she turns around with a gasp, her eyes as wide as saucers. "Hayden, what are you doing in here?"

I know I shouldn't, but I can't help myself. I move in closer, crowding her body with my own. Her breathing slows, becoming heavy and a little ragged. In that moment, I know she wants me. It's only my enormous self-restraint that keeps me from seeing just how far I can push it.

"I dreamt of you last night," I tell her, my voice a soft growl. "And I wake up today, walk out of my room, and here you are, right in front of me like a figment of my imagination. I had to follow you to see if you were real."

Emily bites her lower lip and looks away for a moment, blushing. "I might've thought about you last night too," she admits. She spreads her fingers inches apart to indicate just how much. "Just a little."

Desire courses through my veins as I move in even

closer. "Oh really?" I growl. "And what did you think about?"

She's practically shaking, and the corner of my lips curl up into a grin as she searches for words. "Nothing. Just… our date."

I arch an eyebrow, placing a hand on the small of her back and pulling her closer. "Are you sure that's all?"

"Y-yes."

She's lying, but it doesn't matter, I'll let her off the hook.

"I had a great time talking to you yesterday," I say, "… and you know, after."

"After?" Emily asks breathlessly. The smell of her desire is in the air, her warm lush body making me hot as hell. "What do you mean—"

I seem to lose control of myself. If we get caught, damn it all. At least I can go home a happy man. I close in, kissing her passionately and with a growl, I pull her to me by her hips. The feeling of her ass under my hands is electric and my cock surges to full hardness, sand-wiched between our bodies.

She moans, her hands moving over my shoulders to tangle in my hair at the nape of my neck. Spreading her legs slightly, she grinds against me, she already wants it hard and deep, and I'm more than happy to oblige.

Kissing down her neck, nibbling and licking, I move

my hands to cup her breasts, teasing her already hard nipples. I slip the strap of her cami tank top off her shoulder and suck her nipple into my mouth, teasing it in tight circles with the tip of my tongue. "Oh god, Hayden," she whines in my ear, trying to be good but unable to help herself. "Hayden...."

I move up, whispering in her ear. "As hot as it is to hear you say my name like that, we need to be quiet. Can you be quiet for me?"

Emily nods, biting her lip to keep herself silent and I lower back down, sucking her right nipple into my mouth, rubbing and pinching the other. Pulling back, I catch her eye. "Emily, I need to touch you. Fuck, can I touch you?"

She dips her head once, and I slip a hand up the loose leg of her shorts, cupping her pussy through her cotton panties. She's hot and wet, and she feels like warm caramel almost. "Mmm, you're soaked."

Emily nods wordlessly in reply as I slip a finger into her panties, pulling them to the side and run my finger across her delicate folds. Emily can't hold back her soft moan, her hips pressing forward and searching for more. I ease my finger into her, curling up towards her front wall. In and out, I press, adding another finger to fill her and using my thumb to rub across her clit. "Hayden, I'm so close. Don't stop."

I feel her tight pussy squeeze as she gets ready to come and just in time, I cover her mouth with mine, muffling her cries as I feel her coat my fingers with her orgasm. I keep swiping my thumb across her clit, prolonging her pleasure until she bucks at me, letting out a big happy sigh. When it's over, I pull back, looking into those wide, sexy eyes. "That was the sexiest fucking thing I've ever seen."

Emily smiles, shaken by the intensity of what just happened. "Wow... that was..."

She stops mid-sentence as she realizes I've moved my fingers from inside her to my mouth, sucking at her juices. I meet her eye and let her watch as I run my tongue around and around. "Sexiest fucking thing I've ever tasted too."

She smiles, moving forward to kiss me. After a moment, she seems to remember where we are. "Shit. McKayla and Brad are gonna be here any minute!"

I help her adjust her clothes back and just as I meet her lips with mine for a goodbye kiss, the door opens behind us.

"Girrrrlll..." a high falsetto voice gives me half a second of warning, and I turn around and see the pink–haired pinup and Brad, both of them grinning at us with matching raised eyebrows.

"Alright, I'm McKayla, that's Brad, and you are **not** supposed to fucking be in here," she says looking at me with a glare that could kill.

Brad smirks, his eyes glued on my crotch a little too

much for my comfort. "Or be *fucking* in here."

Emily is turning redder by the moment, stammering to cover up what just happened. "No, uh… we were just talking about our date last night."

"Don't even try it, horny pussy. Even I know what a just-o'd woman looks like. And it's… that." He pauses, moving his hands around indicating Emily's entire body. "I can't blame you though, he's hotter than a habanero tamale."

I have to do the right thing and try and keep Emily out of trouble. "Look, I'm sorry. It's not Emily's fault, I just snuck in here to talk to her. There's no need to cause any trouble with Meredith."

McKayla and Brad look at each other, then McKayla speaks up. "What are your intentions with my girl here?"

Her girl? Interesting. "Uh, aren't we all here to see if we're a match? Last night was great and I just wanted to tell her that. One thing led to another, just not exactly what you're thinking."

McKayla gives me an appraising staredown for a moment, and I can tell she's running me through her bullshit detector. With a nod, she steps away from the door. "Uh huh. Well, y'all got damn lucky there's no cameras in here or y'all would be all over the production studio right now. From here on out, do the dates, see if you're a match, and skip the impromptu outings. Capiche?"

I nod once at McKayla and turn to Emily. "Sorry about that. I'll see you in a bit for our date?"

She nods and I figure we're already in deep, so I lean in, meeting her eyes and cover her mouth with a quick kiss. Moving to her ear, I whisper. "Sexiest fucking thing ever."

With a smile, I slip out the door, hearing the immediate chatter start behind me as McKayla and Brad laughingly interrogate Emily. "Bitch! Tell me everything…."

As I make it down the hall, I can't help but smile. That was awesome and ended better than I could've imagined. Well, it could have ended slightly better, and that would be to have my still aching cock filling her body until she moans my name in my ear. We'll have to be more careful next time. I head out to meet the rest of suitors and the production team for today's date setup.

Coming October 20th!

Join my mailing list and receive 2 FREE ebooks! You'll also be the first to know of new releases, sales, and giveaways.

ABOUT THE AUTHOR

Connect with Lauren Landish

www.laurenlandish.com

admin@laurenlandish.com

Made in the USA
San Bernardino, CA
13 January 2018